# JUDY AND
# THE BEAST

# GOOSEBUMPS®
## HALL OF HORRORS

#1 CLAWS!
#2 NIGHT OF THE GIANT EVERYTHING
#3 SPECIAL EDITION: THE FIVE MASKS OF DR. SCREEM
#4 WHY I QUIT ZOMBIE SCHOOL
#5 DON'T SCREAM!
#6 THE BIRTHDAY PARTY OF NO RETURN

# GOOSEBUMPS®
## MOST WANTED

#1 PLANET OF THE LAWN GNOMES
#2 SON OF SLAPPY
#3 HOW I MET MY MONSTER
#4 FRANKENSTEIN'S DOG
#5 DR. MANIAC WILL SEE YOU NOW
#6 CREATURE TEACHER: FINAL EXAM
#7 A NIGHTMARE ON CLOWN STREET
#8 NIGHT OF THE PUPPET PEOPLE
#9 HERE COMES THE SHAGGEDY
#10 THE LIZARD OF OZ

SPECIAL EDITION #1 ZOMBIE HALLOWEEN
SPECIAL EDITION #2 THE 12 SCREAMS OF CHRISTMAS
SPECIAL EDITION #3 TRICK OR TRAP
SPECIAL EDITION #4 THE HAUNTER

# GOOSEBUMPS®
## SLAPPYWORLD

#1 SLAPPY BIRTHDAY TO YOU
#2 ATTACK OF THE JACK!
#3 I AM SLAPPY'S EVIL TWIN
#4 PLEASE DO NOT FEED THE WEIRDO
#5 ESCAPE FROM SHUDDER MANSION
#6 THE GHOST OF SLAPPY
#7 IT'S ALIVE! IT'S ALIVE!
#8 THE DUMMY MEETS THE MUMMY!
#9: REVENGE OF THE INVISIBLE BOY
#10: DIARY OF A DUMMY
#11: THEY CALL ME THE NIGHT HOWLER!
#12: MY FRIEND SLAPPY
#13: MONSTER BLOOD IS BACK
#14: FIFTH-GRADE ZOMBIE

# GOOSEBUMPS®

Also available as ebooks

NIGHT OF THE LIVING DUMMY
DEEP TROUBLE
MONSTER BLOOD
THE HAUNTED MASK
ONE DAY AT HORRORLAND
THE CURSE OF THE MUMMY'S TOMB
BE CAREFUL WHAT YOU WISH FOR
SAY CHEESE AND DIE!
THE HORROR AT CAMP JELLYJAM
HOW I GOT MY SHRUNKEN HEAD
THE WEREWOLF OF FEVER SWAMP
A NIGHT IN TERROR TOWER
WELCOME TO DEAD HOUSE
WELCOME TO CAMP NIGHTMARE
GHOST BEACH
THE SCARECROW WALKS AT MIDNIGHT
YOU CAN'T SCARE ME!
RETURN OF THE MUMMY
REVENGE OF THE LAWN GNOMES
PHANTOM OF THE AUDITORIUM
VAMPIRE BREATH
STAY OUT OF THE BASEMENT
A SHOCKER ON SHOCK STREET
LET'S GET INVISIBLE!
NIGHT OF THE LIVING DUMMY 2
NIGHT OF THE LIVING DUMMY 3
THE ABOMINABLE SNOWMAN OF PASADENA
THE BLOB THAT ATE EVERYONE
THE GHOST NEXT DOOR
THE HAUNTED CAR
ATTACK OF THE GRAVEYARD GHOULS
PLEASE DON'T FEED THE VAMPIRE
THE HEADLESS GHOST
THE HAUNTED MASK 2
BRIDE OF THE LIVING DUMMY
ATTACK OF THE JACK-O'-LANTERNS

## ALSO AVAILABLE:

IT CAME FROM OHIO!: MY LIFE AS A WRITER by R.L. Stine

# JUDY AND THE BEAST

# R.L. STINE

SCHOLASTIC INC.

Goosebumps book series created by Parachute Press, Inc.
Copyright © 2021 by Scholastic Inc.

ISBN 978-1-338-75214-4

10  9  8  7  6  5  4  3  2  1          21  22  23  24  25

Printed in the U.S.A.   40
First printing 2021

# SLAPPY HERE, EVERYONE.

Welcome to My World.

Yes, it's *SlappyWorld*—you're only *screaming* in it! Hahaha.

One thing to remember: Don't call me Dummy, dummy. I don't like name-calling, you *jerk*! Haha.

I have a sunny personality. I face every day with a smile. I face every *night* with a smile, too. Maybe that's because my lips are painted on! Haha.

I'm so bright, I have to wear sunglasses when I look in the mirror!

How smart am I? I'm so smart, I can count from one to ten without moving my lips! I'm so smart, I know how this sentence will end before I even *say* it! Hahaha!

Some people think that I'm evil and mean. How *dare* they say that! I only have lovely, sweet thoughts. And if you don't agree with me, I'd like to bite your face till your head explodes! Hahaha!

I'm a nice guy. If you forget that, I'll bite you till you remember how nice I am!

1

Speaking of *nice,* I have a nice scary story for you. It's called *Judy and the Beast.*

It's about a girl. Guess what her name is.

Judy?

Good guess.

Does Judy meet a terrifying beast in the forest?

I'll let her tell the story.

It's just one more frightening tale from *SlappyWorld*!

I jumped and cried out as the monster roared into my face. I shot both hands up and tried to push it away.

"Get back, Ira!" I shouted. "You're not funny."

My brother laughed and lowered his carved wooden monster to his side. He took a step back. Then he waved the monster at me again. "It's pretty awesome, don't you think, Judy?"

"You're *sick*," I said. "You think it's normal to spend all your time in the garage building monsters?"

He nodded. "Yeah. Normal."

I shoved the tall wooden thing out of my way and crossed to the open garage door. "Sick," I repeated.

I turned to the shelves against the wall. "Look at them all. A dozen monsters. And what do you do with them, Ira? You don't put on puppet shows or anything, or show them off to people. Your

3

monsters just sit there on the shelves, staring at the driveway."

Ira laughed again. He has an annoying laugh. Like gravel scraping in his throat. "They're waiting to attack," he said. "When I give the signal, my monsters will take over the town."

He picked up a small square of sandpaper and began smoothing it over his monster's wooden back. Our garage has every kind of tool and lots of supplies. A lathe. Two different kinds of saws. A whole wall of hammers and pliers and chisels and things that are a total mystery to me.

That's because our dad is a carpenter.

He does useful work. He doesn't use his tools to build monster after monster.

"Ira, you're fifteen," I said. "Why don't you play video games like everyone else in your class? Or, if you want to build stuff, why don't you build model airplanes or cars?"

"I like monsters," he replied. He raised the monster and started to gently sand one of its long ears.

I shrugged. "Yeah. Okay. I get it, Ira. Sulphur Falls is a boring place to live. You need a hobby."

"It's not just a hobby," he said. He carried the monster to the shelves and set it down next to one of the others. "These are going to be valuable someday."

He straightened a fat, fanged creation and wiped dust off its broad head. "I'm going to start a monster YouTube channel and sell them."

Clouds rolled over the sun, and the light dimmed in the garage. It was spring, but the breezes coming down from the mountain felt as chilly as winter.

I straightened my sweater and hugged myself in the sudden cold. "You know what?" I said. "Your monsters would look better if you painted their faces. Why don't you let me do it? You know I love to paint. I could make them a lot creepier."

He shook his head. "No way, Judy. Forget about that. I think they're scarier *without* faces. You have to use your imagination."

I opened my mouth to argue with him, but I heard someone calling my name. I turned and saw Dad striding from the house.

Dad is short and round and white-haired, even though he isn't that old. His friends in town call him Walrus because his white mustache droops down the sides of his mouth like walrus tusks.

Dad's stomach bounced under his overalls as he walked. He wears denim overalls with lots of pockets for his tools, and red-and-black flannel shirts. And the front of him is usually covered in sawdust, so it looks like he has terrible dandruff.

"Hey, Dad," I said. "What's up?"

He stopped at the garage door. The wind ruffled his white hair. "Hi, Judy," he said. "I'm afraid I have bad news."

5

# 2

Before we get to Dad's bad news, I should start out by telling you about me and my family and all that beginning-story stuff.

You probably figured out my name is Judy. Judy Glassman. I'm twelve and my brother, Ira The Monster Maker, is fifteen.

After our parents split up, Mom decided to move to England. We visit her as often as we can. Dad moved Ira and me here to Sulphur Falls, Wyoming.

It's a tiny ski town at the bottom of Black Rock Mountain. The mountain is snow-covered most of the year, and the skiing is good. Otherwise, why would people come here?

Dad moved us to get back to his roots. He grew up on a ranch in Wyoming. He wanted us to have a fresh start. And he argued, "People in small towns need carpenters, too."

Ira and I wanted to stay back East. We didn't want to leave our friends. But how could we argue with Dad? Besides, Ira and I are not exactly timid. I'm not bragging, but I'd say we're always up for a new adventure.

And living in this tiny town at the foot of Black Rock Mountain is definitely an adventure. With the sun behind it, the mountain's shadow falls over the entire town.

It's dark most of the day, and the mountain air is at least ten degrees colder than anywhere else. I'm so happy that spring has come around because it means a few warm days before the cold returns.

Okay, that's it for beginning-story stuff. Now let's get back to Dad.

I followed him into the house. We have a wood-burning stove in the middle of the kitchen, and it keeps the room warm and toasty. We sat down across from each other at the breakfast counter.

I tapped my fingers on the white countertop. "Let me have it," I said. "What's your bad news?"

Dad tugged at the sides of his walrus mustache. "Well, you know what happens every spring, Judy," he began. "Time for me to go up to Baker Grendel's house."

I groaned. "Again? Do you really have to go this year?"

He nodded. "You know I do. The snow is melting, and the roads up the mountain are passable. The Grendels are expecting me."

Baker Grendel and his wife, Hilda, have a huge

7

mansion at the top of the mountain. At least, that's what I've heard. I've never seen it.

Dad travels up there every spring to make repairs and do carpentry work for them. He usually stays for a week. One year, he got snowed in and was stuck on the mountain for nearly two weeks.

He ran a hand through his thick, white hair. "Baker and Hilda are strange," he said. "But they pay very well."

I groaned and rolled my eyes. "And I suppose you're taking Ira with you as always?" I said. "You're taking Ira and leaving me behind with Mrs. Hardwell?"

Dad's cheeks turned pink. He knows Mrs. Hardwell and I don't get along. To put it mildly.

Mrs. Hardwell is our housekeeper, and she's always on my case. She's boring and strict and too serious. And she never wants me to have any fun.

Dad avoided my stare. He glanced out the kitchen window to the backyard. "Yes," he said finally. "I'm taking Ira."

I slammed my fist on the table. "No fair!" I shouted. "No fair, Dad."

"Judy, please—"

"You take Ira every year," I said. "It's my turn. I want to go, too. How can you be so unfair?"

"Ira helps me with the work," Dad said. "He knows the tools from working on his wooden monsters."

"I know tools—" I started.

He raised a hand, motioning for me to stop. "I can't take you both," he said. "The ride up to the mountaintop is just too treacherous. You know I can't even take the jeep. The melting snow makes the dirt road too slippery. I have to take a horse and wagon. You'd hate it, Judy."

"Try me," I said. "I won't hate it. I promise, Dad." I could feel my anger tightening my throat. Dad's reasons didn't make sense.

Why couldn't I go? Why did it always have to be Ira?

"I don't want to stay with Mrs. Hardwell," I shouted. "She's horrid!"

A voice behind me made me gasp. "You can't mean that, Judy." Mrs. Hardwell appeared at the kitchen door.

She walked in shaking her head. Her short, straight black hair bobbed with her head, and her tiny blackbird eyes were locked on me. A smile spread across her pale narrow face, but I knew it was totally fake.

"Sorry you feel that way," she said. She speaks with a smooth, velvety voice. Also fake. "It's because you think you can run wild when your father isn't here. I have to keep you in line."

Dad's cheeks turned even pinker. They always do when he's embarrassed or stressed. And he hates arguments of any kind. Dad is much more comfortable with a hammer and nails than dealing with people.

I knew I should apologize to Mrs. Hardwell. "Sorry," I muttered. "I . . . I didn't really mean you were horrid. It just . . . slipped out."

Her fake smile faded. "You and I will have a good time together, Judy," she said. "I'm going to teach you how to embroider."

She patted me on the shoulder. Her hand was ice-cold. "You're very artistic," she said. "You'll like embroidery."

I groaned. "Kill me now," I murmured.

I don't know if she heard me or not. But Dad did. "Maybe next year—" he started.

But I cut him off. "If Ira can go, I can go," I said.

He shook his head. "I wish Ira could stay home, but I need his help. The Grendels are very strange people. You'd hate them, Judy." He lowered his voice. "And there's one other thing I didn't tell you . . ."

I narrowed my eyes at him. "What's that?"

"There are rumors . . ." he whispered.

"Huh? Rumors?"

His blue eyes locked on mine. "Frightening rumors about an inhuman beast," he said. "A deadly creature on the prowl up there."

I tossed back my head and laughed. "A beast? Nice one, Dad. I'm really going to believe that."

# 3

The cart banged and rattled and shook as the horse pulled it up the narrow, twisting dirt path toward the mountaintop. I could hear the horse stumbling in the mud. I could hear my dad urging it on.

"Is he going to make it?" Ira's voice cracked. He sounded scared.

The wagon jerked to one side, then tilted hard to the other side.

I felt every bump.

Judy Glassman never takes no for an answer.

I was hiding in one of Dad's canvas supply bags at the back of the wagon. It seemed like a good idea early this morning. Now I wasn't so sure.

I knew when I popped out, Dad wouldn't be happy. But I knew he would get over it, and the three of us could have a good time. Unfortunately, it turned out the ride was just as treacherous as Dad had said.

And, as much as I tried to tell myself everything would be okay, I couldn't hide my fear from myself. I was plenty scared!

It was all I could do not to break out whistling.

You see, I have this very weird habit. I always start to whistle when I'm feeling tense or afraid. Or whenever I'm in trouble.

I can't explain it. I usually don't even know I'm doing it. I just start whistling. It drives Ira crazy. Ha. Maybe that's why I do it! And now as I bounced inside the canvas bag, feeling every bump and jolt of the wagon, I had to grit my teeth hard to keep myself from whistling. I definitely didn't want Dad to find me till we reached the top of the mountain.

Up at the front of the cart, I could hear Dad and Ira talking. They had to shout over the clatter of the wagon wheels.

"Baker Grendel can be frightening if you don't know him," Dad was saying.

Ira laughed. "Even if you *do* know him!" he exclaimed. "I remember the first time I met him. I was *terrified*."

"He's so big, so heavy," Dad said.

"Yeah. Scary," Ira agreed.

*Just how scary can he be?* I wondered.

Inside the canvas bag, I bounced hard as the wagon stopped. I heard creaks and scraping sounds. Then the hard *thuds* as Dad and Ira jumped off the wagon.

My heart started to pound. Almost time for me to appear—my big surprise.

I heard their footsteps leading away from the wagon. Silence for a short while. Then I heard a woman's greeting: "Oh, hello. You have arrived."

"How have you been, Hilda?" I heard Dad ask.

"It was a long winter," she replied. She had a high, little-girl voice.

I raised my hands to the top of the canvas bag. *Showtime!*

I pushed open the bag and raised my head a few inches above the opening.

I saw a massive stone house that seemed to stretch forever. I waited for my eyes to adjust to the light. Then I turned to the wide front doors and saw my dad and Ira standing on the low front stoop.

Their backs were to me as they talked with Hilda Grendel. She was an older woman with short gray hair and a round rosy face. She wore a long gray housedress that came down nearly to her ankles.

Hilda was telling them about last winter on the mountaintop. As she talked, she gestured with her hands. She swept them from side to side as she spoke about the powerful winds and the damage they had done.

"There's some serious repair work here," she told Dad. "I'm sorry to say there's even some repairs that have to be made on the roof."

Dad kept nodding his head as she filled him in. Ira shifted his weight from leg to leg. He stretched his back. I heard him say something about the long, bumpy ride.

"Well, come in," Hilda said, backing up into the doorway. "Baker is in his private dining room. He's having an early dinner. You know how he is about his meals. I would never disturb him while he's eating. You'll see him soon."

They started into the house—but then stopped.

I gulped when I saw Hilda's dark eyes. She gazed over Dad's shoulder to the wagon. She saw me poking my head out of the supply bag.

She uttered a short laugh and pointed at me. "I think you have a stowaway," she told Dad.

Dad and Ira spun around. Their eyes went wide, and they both gasped in shock as I pulled the bag down to my knees and started to climb out.

"Surprise!" I shouted.

Everyone froze for a moment. And then Dad's cheeks darkened to a deep red. "Judy," he said finally. "I think you've made a bad mistake."

The house was surprisingly dark. The walls of the enormous front room were painted deep green. The room was filled with black-leather furniture: two long couches and several wide armchairs all facing one another in a rectangle.

Heavy drapes were pulled shut across the front windows. The only light came from a few dim floor lamps beside the black-leather couches.

We followed Hilda across the room. Tall portraits of stern-looking old people posing stiffly in old-fashioned clothing stared out at us. Hilda stopped at a steep, winding stairway in a hall at the back of the room.

A suit of armor stood erect against the hallway wall. The metal was dull, with green stains on the chest and helmet. I could see it hadn't been polished in a long while.

An elk head was mounted on the wall above the suit of armor. The elk had a stunned look on its face, as if it was surprised to have ended up there.

*Everything is old and dark and creepy. It's like a haunted mansion in a horror movie.*

That was my thought as I gazed up the marble stairs.

I wondered if that was one reason Dad never wanted me to come here. He should know I'm not the scaredy-cat type. I don't scream at horror movies, and I think Halloween haunted houses are funny, not scary.

"I'm sure you and Ira know the way to your rooms," Hilda told my dad. She turned to me. "Judy, pick any room across from theirs. They are all empty."

We started up the marble staircase. Dad led the way. Ira waited until I caught up with him. Then he bumped me in the side. "Why did you come, Judy?" he whispered.

"Huh?" The anger on his face surprised me.

He brought his face close to mine and whispered, "Does Mrs. Hardwell know you're here?"

"I left her a note," I said.

Ira sighed. "Our time at the Grendels' house is special for Dad and me. Why did you have to horn in and spoil it for me?"

My mouth dropped open. I never dreamed Ira would be this upset that I had decided to come along.

It took me a little while to find my voice. "Why don't *you* try staying home with Mrs. Hardwell and learning embroidery?" I snapped.

He made a growling sound and hurried past me to catch up with Dad.

We stopped at the second-floor landing. A long hall with a deep purple carpet stretched in front of us. More tall portraits of unhappy-looking men and women lined the walls. Tiny lamps shaped like torches flickered all the way down the hall.

"It's like a movie set," I said to Dad.

He scratched his head. "Not really. I installed all these lamps. It didn't remind me of a movie."

He stopped at an open door halfway down the long hall. "This is my room," he told me. "Why don't you take that one?" He pointed to the doorway right across the hall.

I started toward it, but he grabbed my arm to stop me. "I know you like to wander around and explore new places," he said. "But we should talk about Baker Grendel before you do that."

I blinked. "Talk about him?"

Dad nodded. "There are some things you should know."

# 5

My room felt more cheerful than the rest of the house. For one thing, the walls were white, not some dark, drab color. Since I'm an artist, color is very important to me.

I think I'm more sensitive to color than most people. If I had to live here, all the dark walls and carpet and furniture would totally bring me down.

Also, my room had two tall windows with no drapes or curtains. The sun was lowering behind the trees, and amber light washed into the room. That cheered me up a lot.

I peered down from the window. My room must have been at the back of the mansion. I could see rolling lawns of tall grass and behind them a thick forest, tangled trees shimmering in the dying sunlight.

The king-sized bed had a tall headboard, six big pillows, and was covered in a lacy pink quilt. A light-wood dresser stood against one wall beside a small desk.

I tried my phone, but, of course, it didn't work. I had a feeling there wouldn't be cell service this high up the mountain. Did Hilda and Baker Grendel have landlines? Computers? Internet?

A knock on the door made me spin around. A short bald man in a dark suit stood in the hall holding the canvas supply bag. He had a sad face with dark circles around his eyes. He was a little stooped over, and the suit sagged on him.

"My name is Harvard, miss," he said. "I brought up your things."

"Oh, thank you," I said. I took the bag from him.

"We haven't seen you here before," he said.

I shook my head. "No. It's my first time."

He narrowed his sad, watery eyes at me. "Be careful, miss," he said, his chin quivering. "Be careful."

"Oh. Okay." I didn't know what to say. And then I said, "What should I be careful about?" He turned around and left without answering me.

For a long moment, I stood there staring at the empty doorway. "Strange," I muttered. "Seriously strange."

It didn't take long to unpack the bag. I didn't bring much. Some sweaters and slacks and my winter parka. And, of course, I squeezed my easel and paints into the bag.

I set the easel up beside the windows. I've never painted any landscapes. But I imagined the back lawn with the forest behind it would be interesting to paint.

19

My stomach growled. I was starting to get a little hungry.

I looked for Dad across the hall, but he wasn't in his room. I stopped at Ira's room, too, but he wasn't there.

I decided they must have gone downstairs.

The smooth, wooden banister was cool under my hand as I followed the curving stairs down. I tried to ignore the stern, unpleasant faces staring at me from the paintings on the walls.

I walked past the suit of armor and stepped into the dark front room. "Dad? Ira?" My voice echoed off the walls.

I knew they wouldn't go eat without me. I thought maybe they were somewhere with Hilda.

But which way to go?

Hallways stretched at both sides of the room. I gazed from one to the other. I had never been in a house with two *wings* before.

*Just pick one, Judy,* I told myself. *Maybe you'll run into them.*

I chose the hall at the other end, away from the curving stairway. This hall appeared to stretch for miles. It was as dimly lit as the other, with dark green walls and an even darker carpet.

I wanted to shout for Dad and Ira. But then I thought maybe it wasn't a good idea.

I had passed several rooms, the doors all closed, when I stopped. I sniffed the air. I smelled the pleasant aroma of food.

It came from the room on my left. I turned to the closed door. Was this Baker Grendel's private dining room?

Probably. The aroma of food floated over me.

I stepped up close to the door. I jumped when I heard a noise.

An animal growl.

Inside the room.

I pressed my ear against the wood. And heard loud snarls. A deep animal growl. Wet gulping sounds.

*Slurp slurrrp slurrrp chomp!*

I pictured a big animal, snarling and growling and devouring its dinner.

But how could that be?

What was going *on* in there?

Back home, I didn't believe my dad when he told me about a wild beast that was on the loose up here. I didn't believe him then, and I didn't believe him now.

What a laugh.

As I said, Dad is the worst liar on earth. His cheeks turn bright pink when he makes up stories like that. And he can't look you in the face. He'd be a terrible poker player. He always gives away everything he's thinking.

But how to explain the disgusting sounds I was hearing in the dining room?

Could it really be Baker Grendel eating like that? Was that why he ate alone in a private dining room?

I knew I should turn around, go back down the hall, and find Dad and Ira. But I was frozen there by the door, listening to the chomping and growling.

I had to know who or what was making that noise. I had to see with my own eyes.

My hand trembled as I grabbed the doorknob. I started to turn it . . .

But my hand flew off and I let out a scream as the door swung open in my face.

"Hey—!" I cried.

The heavy door shot open with such force it sent me stumbling backward. I hit the wall. Struggled to catch my breath. And stared at the big, wild-haired man in the doorway.

His dark eyes blinked several times. I think he was as startled as I was.

His wiry white hair spiked up from his head in all directions, as if he'd been struck by lightning. He held a white linen napkin in one hand and used it to mop the orange sauce from his long white beard. He also had orange and brown food stains on the front of his baggy white shirt.

"I-I-I—" I stammered.

He was a giant, so wide he filled the doorway. He gave his beard one final wipe with the napkin, then narrowed his eyes at me. "I *thought* I heard someone outside the door," he said. His voice was low and gravelly, and seemed to come from deep in his bulging chest.

"Y-yes," I stammered. I could feel my face go hot and knew I was blushing. "I-I—"

"You must be Judy," he boomed. "My wife told me about you."

I nodded. "Yes. I wanted to come with my dad this year," I said, finally finding my voice.

He covered his mouth with the napkin and burped loudly. "I'm just finishing my dinner," he said.

*So that really was him devouring his food like a wild animal?*

"I'd invite you in," he continued, "but I prefer to dine alone. I'll come greet you and your family after you have your dinner with Hilda."

I opened my mouth to answer. But he closed the door before I could get a sound out.

I stood there for a long moment with my back against the wall. My thoughts were spinning through my head. I kept picturing the splotches of orange sauce in his white beard. His hair so wild and unbrushed. His dark eyes studying me.

Dad said that Baker was weird. He wasn't kidding about that!

Finally, I turned and made my way to the front of the house. I found Ira standing at the bottom of the stairs beneath the elk head. I trotted up to him. "Ira, listen to me—" I started.

"Where were you?" he asked. "Dad and I were looking for you."

I pointed to the other hall. "Down there. I was at Baker Grendel's private dining room. I-I couldn't believe it."

Ira frowned at me. "You're not supposed to go in that wing."

"He was eating his dinner," I said, ignoring Ira's words. "It sounded like a wild animal was in

24

there." I had to take a breath. "It . . . it sounded like a tiger devouring a live pig or something."

To my surprise, Ira tossed his head back and laughed.

"Huh?" I cried. "What's so funny?"

"You'll find out," he said.

"This old mansion took twenty years to build," Baker said. "Can you imagine the builders carrying the limestone up to the mountaintop, stone by stone?"

He grabbed a handful of red grapes from the bowl on the table beside him and stuffed them into his mouth. Juice ran down his beard as he chewed.

"Bringing the lumber up here must have also been a nearly impossible task," Dad said.

Baker nodded. "Some of the lumber came from the trees in the forest. But most of it had to be carried here."

We were sitting in a den after dinner. Baker filled a wide armchair. He kept reaching for the grapes beside the chair.

Hilda sat across from him, tilting up and down gently in a tall wooden rocker. Dad, Ira, and I were seated together, facing them on a long couch. The couch was so deep, my feet didn't touch the floor.

A fire crackled and danced in a wide stone fireplace. I could hear gusts of wind rattling the tall windows across from it.

The walls were covered with trophies of animal horns. Elk horns maybe.

Hilda saw me staring up at the horns. "Baker's grandfather was quite the hunter," she said, smiling at her husband. "Those antlers are from elks he bagged."

I pictured the animals all running free in the mountain forest. And I shuddered at the thought of how they were killed.

"I try to keep my ancestors alive here in this house," Baker said. "Judy, I'm sure you noticed their portraits on the walls in the front?"

I nodded. "Yes. Nice." *Awkward.* I didn't know what to say.

Baker spit out a grape pit. "They weren't exactly a fun bunch," he said, snickering. He turned to Dad. "I feel this place has to be rebuilt every year. Every spring, there's a lot to repair and maintain." He sighed. "As I'm sure Hilda told you, this year, there was even storm damage on the roof."

"I am pleased to help out every spring," Dad said. He tapped Ira's knee. "And I have Ira to act as an assistant."

Ira smiled but didn't say a word. He and I had been silent the whole time.

*Why does Ira like to come here?* I asked myself. *The old house is definitely creepy. And Baker and Hilda aren't exactly a fun couple.*

"Would anyone like a cup of tea?" Hilda asked, starting to rise from her rocking chair. "I can feel a cold draft from the windows."

Baker raised a hand. "Make it a tall mug. Those little teacups are too small for me."

When Hilda left the room, he turned to me. "I have to talk to you, Judy," he rumbled in his gravelly voice. "It's your first time here, so there are some things I'd like to tell you."

I nodded. "Sorry I interrupted your dinner—" I started.

He raised a hand. "No problem. You don't know the rules." He motioned to the den door. "I really like to keep that wing of the house to myself," he said. "It's where I do my work and where I go to think and be alone."

"Sorry—" I said again.

"I want you to enjoy my shabby old castle up here," he boomed. "But please keep out of that wing. I really need to keep it private."

"No problem," I said.

*What's the big deal anyway?*

"Judy likes to explore," Ira chimed in. "Sometimes she goes on long hikes for miles, and Dad and I have to go search for her."

"That's not true!" I cried. "I don't get lost. I just like to keep going. Besides, how can you get lost in Sulphur Falls? The whole town is about as big as the back lawn here."

"That brings me to my second rule," Baker said. He shoved a bunch of grapes into his mouth and chewed. "It's okay to explore the grounds," he said after swallowing loudly. "But if you go into the forest, don't stray from the path."

"I'll bet there's awesome wildlife in the forest," I said. "I'd love to see—"

"Please listen to what I'm saying," Baker interrupted. "Yes, the forest wildlife is interesting. But don't go off on your own, Judy, and don't go off the path."

He leaned toward me and his smile faded. His dark eyes grew cold. "There are many dangers," he said. "Many dangers. I couldn't be more serious. Many dangers."

I stared back at him, at his intense expression, his dark eyes burning into mine.

Was he trying to scare me?

# 8

I fell asleep quickly. I think the mountain air plus all the tension made me sleepy. I was in the middle of a disturbing dream. I was inside the canvas bag, bouncing in the wagon, and I couldn't get out. The top of the bag was sealed, and I couldn't find an opening no matter how hard I struggled.

I woke up with a short cry. I sat up straight, instantly alert.

Noises outside the windows rose over the steady rush of the wind. Thumps and low cries.

Shaking off the frightening dream, I darted to the window and peered down. It was the middle of the night. Almost total darkness. No moon or stars.

I pressed my hot forehead against the glass and squinted hard. Was that an animal standing so still in the grass? Through the glass, I could hear heavy rustling, like someone pushing through the long row of bushes that bordered the mansion.

But I couldn't see anything. I stepped back from the window. Half asleep, I turned and rushed out the bedroom door. I knew I wasn't thinking clearly. But I am impulsive. I act first, then think later. That's what I'm about.

I just *had* to see what was making those sounds.

My bare feet tapped the hall carpet as I ran to the stairs. The house was dark except for a dim yellow light at the side of the kitchen door.

I fiddled with the locks, fumbling as I turned them one way, then the other. I burst outside into the cold darkness. The wind ruffled my long nightshirt. The chill air forced me totally awake.

The ground was cold and hard with patches of hardened snow dotting the tall grass. Wrapping my arms around me, I turned and ran past the row of low bushes.

My eyes slowly adjusted to the darkness. And came to rest on the animal I had seen from my bedroom window. A tall rabbit, standing upright, long ears straight up above its head. Still and stiff as a statue.

*Rabbits freeze like that when they're frightened,* I knew.

But what was frightening this rabbit?

I didn't have long to find out.

I heard the thunder of heavy footsteps. The wind changed, as if disturbed by something big coming toward me. Even the darkness appeared to shift.

I dropped back as an enormous creature burst out from the low bushes. A black shadow rumbling over the tall grass. So dark I could only see its movement, not the creature itself.

I could hear its heavy breathing, louder than the thud of its footsteps, as it leaped forward on all fours. Its black fur gleamed like a dark light. Its big head was down. I couldn't see its eyes.

*The Beast . . . the Beast . . .*

I held my breath. My legs trembled. My whole body shuddered as the creature heaved right past me. I felt the cold wind off its back. An earthy aroma brushed over me.

The big animal was only a few feet away when the rabbit finally turned. It lowered its front paws to the grass and darted ahead, running in a straight line.

The creature thundered after it, a black blur. It rounded the corner of the house and vanished from my sight.

I finally allowed myself to breathe. Was I whistling? Yes. It took me a few seconds to realize I had started to do my usual whistling. I clapped a hand over my mouth to stop it.

And heard a shrill *squeal.*

A cry of pain cut off instantly.

The big creature had captured its prey.

Silence now. So quiet I could actually hear the rapid pounding of my heart.

Another cold shudder shook my body. My legs trembled so hard, I thought I would fall.

*The Beast . . . the Beast . . .*

I had seen it. It was real.

And now I heard its heavy, plodding footsteps again.

It was coming back. Coming for *me.*

It must have heard my whistling. Or else, it *smelled* me.

I pictured the rabbit standing frozen for too long. And once again, I heard its final squeal in my ears.

I forced my trembling legs to move. I spun away from the sound of the running footsteps and took off. My bare feet slipped in the dew-wet grass.

I caught my balance and, gasping with each breath, ran to the kitchen door.

The creature was coming. The creature was close behind. I could hear it. I could feel its heaviness. I didn't have to turn around and see it.

I burst into the warmth of the kitchen and slammed the door behind me. Then I stood there with my back against the door, panting like an animal . . . panting like the *Beast*.

The rabbit's death squeal repeated in my ears.

*That could have been me.*

It took a long while for my breathing to return to normal. My bare feet were cold and wet against the tile of the kitchen floor. I pushed down my windblown hair with both hands.

"I have to wake up Dad," I murmured to myself. "I have to tell him he was right. There *is* a beast up here. We can't stay here."

I crept through the kitchen, into the hall. The house was completely dark, as dark as the back lawn. A loud *click* made me jump. I realized it was just the fridge clicking on in the kitchen behind me.

I tiptoed across the front room, heading to the stairs.

*Dad told the truth about the Beast,* I thought. *That's why he didn't want me to come here.*

But why did he bring Ira here every year?

Moving unsteadily through the darkness, I passed the front entryway. The stairway was ahead in deep shadow.

I grabbed the banister—then froze.

I heard more clicks. This time from the front of the mansion. And then the squeak of the front door opening. The door banged softly against the wall.

I heard a grunt. A low groan. A cough.

My hand squeezed the banister. I held my breath. Too late to run up the stairs.

Someone—or some*thing* had just entered the house.

# 10

I squinted into the darkness. I could see a figure at the front door. I heard another throaty cough.

The entryway light flashed on. It was a man, a large man dressed all in black. A black wool ski cap hid his face from me.

A burst of wind invaded the room. He closed the door behind him.

I didn't move. Would he see me?

He tugged off the cap. Baker. I could see him clearly now. His wiry hair matted to the sides of his face.

He ran a hand down his beard. Then he stomped mud off his tall boots.

I suddenly realized I'd been holding my breath. I let it out in a long whoosh.

He blinked. I could see the surprise on his face as he turned to me. "Judy?" he boomed in his gravelly voice. "What are you doing down here?"

"I-I-I—" I stammered.

He narrowed his eyes at me. "Were you spying on me?"

I gasped. "No. Of course not," I said. "I heard noises outside and—"

He bent to pull off one of his boots. "You probably heard me," he said.

*Huh? Heard you? No. I heard a giant, four-legged beast.*

He tugged off the second boot and stood it up beside the first. "I go out at night," he said.

He pulled off his black gloves and tucked them into his coat pockets. Then he took a few steps toward me. "I'm not a good sleeper," he said. "I get restless at night. I hope I didn't disturb you."

"N-no," I stammered. "I heard a noise outside my window. I guess it was just you."

"I didn't hear anything else out there," he said. "Just the wind blowing. It gets very windy up here at the mountaintop."

"No. It wasn't the wind—" I started.

"Of course, I had my wool hat pulled down over my ears," he said. "So I couldn't hear much." He squinted at me. "Judy, did you *see* anything?"

"Uh . . . no," I lied.

I didn't want to discuss the Beast with him. I needed to talk to Dad about it. Not Baker.

He took another step closer. "You'd better get used to my late-night habits," he said softly.

It didn't sound like a suggestion. It didn't sound like a warning. It sounded like a threat.

# 11

I raced up the stairs and stopped in front of Dad's bedroom door. I raised my fist and knocked hard.

Silence.

I raised my fist again to the door, but then lowered it. I knew I couldn't wake him by knocking. Dad is a very deep sleeper.

I decided I'd talk to him in the morning.

In my room, I paced back and forth for a long while, waiting for my heartbeats to slow. Waiting for the chills to stop. Waiting to feel normal again.

Finally, I climbed into bed and pulled the covers up to my chin. I shut my eyes and tried not to picture that shadowy blur that thundered inches from me, pursuing the poor, doomed rabbit.

I fell into a restless sleep. I kept waking up, rolling over, forcing myself back to sleep.

The next morning, I pulled on jeans and a sweatshirt and hurried to Dad's room. It was empty. He must have gone down to breakfast.

I headed over to the stairs and nearly bumped into Ira, just leaving his room.

"Hey," I said, "stop." I grabbed his arms and pushed him against the wall.

"What's your problem?" he snapped.

"Listen to me," I said, keeping my voice just above a whisper. "I have to tell you what I saw last night. An enormous creature—it ran right past me. It killed a rabbit, Ira. The Beast. It was the Beast that Dad—"

I stopped talking when I saw that he was laughing. "Wh-what's so funny?" I stammered.

He shook his head. "I'll tell you what's so funny," he said. "You believed Dad."

"I . . . what?"

"You believed Dad, Judy. He made that up about a beast running loose up here. I don't know what made him think of it. But it isn't true. He—"

"But I *saw* it!" I cried. I wanted to wipe the grin off Ira's face.

"Dad knows this is a special time for me when I get to be with him up here," Ira said. "He didn't want you to come and spoil it for me. So he made up a crazy story about a beast."

"But, Ira, listen to me—"

"I don't think he ever expected you to *believe* him," Ira said, and laughed again. "Who would believe a dumb thing like that?"

I took a deep breath. "Ira, I was outside last night. I saw—"

He pressed his hand over my mouth. "I'm serious," he said. "Stop. Don't talk about it."

"Don't talk about *what*?" a voice called.

I turned to see Hilda behind me.

"Uh . . . Don't talk about all the work Dad has to do here this year," Ira said, thinking quickly.

She chuckled. "Yes. Don't worry about him. Your dad enjoys his work."

We followed Hilda down to the kitchen for breakfast. Dad was already seated at the table. He greeted us with a smile. "Hope you two have an appetite. Harvard has made us a feast for breakfast," he said, pointing to the platter in the middle of the table. "Blueberry pancakes with eggs and sausages."

I gripped my stomach. I still felt tense from last night.

I was desperate to talk to Dad. But I guessed it would have to wait until after breakfast.

Dad started in on a tall stack of pancakes drenched in syrup on his plate. When he looked up at me, he had syrup dripping down his walrus mustache. "Judy, you look tired. Did you sleep?"

"Not really," I answered. I saw Hilda watching me from the end of the breakfast table. I didn't say any more.

"This breakfast is awesome!" Ira said. "At home, we don't even have eggs."

Dad swallowed a mouthful of pancakes. "You told me you like cereal for breakfast," he said.

Ira frowned. "Every morning?"

"We don't have breakfast like this every morning," Hilda said. "This is a special welcome breakfast."

I heard noises in the hall. And then Baker's cheery shout: "Good morning, everyone."

Baker strode into the room wearing a maroon sweatsuit. His hair shot out in all directions. Grinning, he gave us a big wave.

And then I cried out in alarm. And gaped at the enormous black creature that came bursting into the kitchen from behind him. Its paws thundering over the floor, it came charging at us, head lowered to attack.

The Beast! The Beast—in the house!

# 12

Baker let out a booming laugh. "Judy, that's quite a scream. You haven't met Aurora yet, have you!"

The big beast ran over to Hilda, and she reached out a hand to pet his gigantic head.

"Aurora, say hi to Judy," Baker said. "She's our new guest."

The creature didn't obey. Instead, he raised his head and loudly sniffed the food on the table.

My head was spinning. "It . . . it's a dog?" I managed to choke out.

Ira laughed. "Did you think Aurora was a horse? Of *course* he's a dog."

I could feel my face go hot, and I knew I was blushing. "I-I—"

"Aurora is a Neapolitan mastiff," Baker said. "Maybe the biggest breed of dog on earth." He walked over to the dog and smoothed both hands back over its big face. "I like a big dog."

Aurora walked up to my chair. He raised his head to sniff me. Then he licked the back of my hand with a wide pink tongue.

"He can be very gentle when he wants to be," Baker said. "But be careful, Judy. The dog weighs one hundred fifty pounds! And if he decides he doesn't like you . . ."

Baker grabbed a pancake off the table and shoved it into the big dog's mouth. Aurora gobbled it down, chewing noisily.

I saw Ira grinning at me across the table. Okay. Okay. So he was right. I didn't see a beast last night. I saw Aurora.

I felt like a total idiot.

"Aurora and I go for late-night walks all the time," Baker said. "Didn't you see him with me last night, Judy?"

"No," I said. "I didn't know—"

Dad squinted at me. "You were out last night?" he asked.

I nodded. "I couldn't sleep."

"I thought you saw Aurora when you came to my dining room last night," Baker said. "He and I share every meal."

Now I felt like an even bigger jerk.

It wasn't Baker making those disgusting eating noises I had heard through the dining room door. It was Aurora.

So there was no beast. Dad told me about the Beast to frighten me.

But that was so unlike him. With his cheeks always turning pink, Dad is such a bad liar. He never ever makes up stories.

Why did he make up the one about a beast?

# SLAPPY HERE, EVERYONE.

Judy has a wild imagination.

How could she mistake Aurora for a beast?

After all, Aurora is big and furry and heavy and hard-breathing. And a beast, on the other hand, is big and furry and heavy and hard-breathing! Haha.

Sure, Aurora ate that rabbit. But I think Judy should apologize to the dog.

Aurora is entitled to a midnight snack, isn't he? And just because he likes his meat *rare* doesn't make him a beast.

Is there really a beast at the Grendels' house?

Let me give you a hint. This *is* a horror story— isn't it?

Hahaha!

# 13

After breakfast it seemed everyone had somewhere to go but me.

Dad decided to start the shingle work on the roof and asked Ira to come help him. Baker said he would be working in his office. Hilda said she worked there, too, as his secretary.

I was still at the table when Harvard began to clear the dishes. He wore a crisp white apron over his black suit. His expression was as sad as ever, like a sorrowful hound dog. And the dark circles around his eyes seemed even darker.

"The pancakes were awesome, Harvard," I said.

He nodded. A tight smile crossed his face for just a second. "Would you like a cooking lesson this morning, Miss Judy?" he asked.

I blinked. Did he know that I had nothing planned for the day?

"Well . . . sure," I said finally.

"I'm making a Niçoise salad and a mushroom tart for lunch, and you can help me."

"Sounds like fun," I said.

I'm not exactly handy in the kitchen. Actually, I've never tried to cook anything. Mrs. Hardwell prepares all our meals.

After the dishes were put away, Harvard began pulling ingredients from the kitchen pantry. The tall pantry shelves reached to the ceiling. The pantry was bigger than my room back home.

"We need to bring in a good supply of food," Harvard explained. "Because of the snow in the winter, we can't go down to shop for months at a time."

He gave me a large knife and set me up with romaine lettuce. "Shred it for the salad," he said. "I'm going to work on the dough for the tart."

We worked in silence for a while. The knife was very sharp, and I worked carefully.

After several minutes, the silence grew awkward. "How long have you worked here?" I asked him.

He uttered a sigh. "Longer than you can imagine," he said. "I came with the house."

I stopped chopping. "What do you mean?"

"I worked for Baker's father. When he died, I stayed on with Baker."

I studied him. "So I guess you like the job?"

He started to grate a block of cheese. "I don't know any other," he said softly.

"Don't you get lonely up here?" I asked. I immediately regretted the question. Was I being too nosey?

He didn't answer. He kept his eyes on the cheese grater as it scraped the wedge of cheese.

"What does Baker do?" I asked.

Okay. So I'm nosey. So sue me.

"Hard to say," Harvard answered, still avoiding my eyes.

"No. Really," I insisted. "What is his job? What does he do?"

Harvard picked up a long-bladed knife and held it over the cheese wedge. "Better not to ask questions, Miss Judy," he said, lowering his voice to a whisper.

"What did you say?" I wasn't sure I had heard him correctly.

"It's risky," he said. "Questions can be risky."

*Risky?*

He lowered the knife to the cheese—and I saw it slip.

The blade cut deep into the back of Harvard's hand.

He didn't scream or cry out at all. He just blinked a few times and murmured, "Oh."

I stared at the cut, a straight line sliced deep in the skin.

I stared and felt a wave of shock roll down my body. My mouth dropped open as I studied the back of his hand.

He didn't bleed.

The cut didn't bleed at all.

# 14

Dad and Ira came in for lunch. I tried to tell them about Harvard and the cut on his hand that didn't bleed. But the two of them were talking a mile a minute about the work on the roof. I couldn't get a word in.

When we started to eat the salad, they complimented me on the good job I had done shredding the lettuce.

I knew they were kind of making fun of me. But I didn't want to turn it into an argument. I wanted Ira to come for a walk with me in the forest.

He glanced across the table at Dad. "I can't," Ira said. "I have to help on the roof."

"Where are Hilda and Baker?" I asked.

"They usually eat lunch in their private dining room," Dad said. "That way, they can get back to work quickly."

"What does Baker do?" I asked. "Harvard wouldn't tell me."

"It's complicated," he said.

I squinted at him. "Complicated?"

"Kind of," Dad said. "It's hard to say what he does exactly. He is very mysterious."

"Everyone around here is mysterious," I said. "I can't get a straight answer to any question."

"Maybe you ask too many questions," Ira said. Then he laughed.

Was that supposed to be a joke?

The narrow dirt trail led in a straight line from the tall grass at the back of the house into the tangled trees of the forest. The ground was frozen from the cold. My boots cracked over patches of thin ice.

My breath steamed in front of me as I walked. I zipped my parka up to the fur collar. Above me, the sky was gray. Low clouds formed a dark blanket over the sun.

It had snowed a little in the morning. The air still felt heavy and wet, and I thought it might start snowing again.

I stopped at the edge of the trees and watched a large red falcon swoop down over the tall grass. The bird had its eye on something in the grass. It swooped low, picked up a small animal, raised its broad wings, and sailed off with it.

I tightened my hood around my face and followed the path into the trees. The air grew cooler as soon as I stepped into the forest. Gray light washed down through the treetops, dark as evening.

I shivered. It was colder than I'd imagined. I wished Ira had come along.

I thought about turning around and going back to the house. But I really wanted to explore. Maybe I could find something awesome to paint.

A cluster of red and purple wildflowers caught my eye. They swayed from one side to the other, as if dancing to a silent melody.

I reached into my pocket for my phone. I wanted to photograph them. Maybe I could paint them later. I sighed when I realized I'd left my phone in my room.

I studied them for a while. I wanted to remember how the blossom colors blended from red to purple. I felt a deep chill as the wind picked up. A signal to keep moving.

Baker had warned to stay on the dirt path and not wander off into the trees. I guess he was worried about me getting turned around and lost.

I have a very good sense of direction. But I decided to follow his instructions, and I stayed on the narrow path as it zigged and zagged between the tall trees.

I stayed on the path until I saw the cabin.

It stood in a small clearing between two enormous trees. A square cabin. It looked like a brown box with a flat roof. I saw a narrow wooden door in the front and a small window beside it.

Dead brown leaves piled up at one side of the cabin. A garden rake tilted against the other side.

Was someone in there?

*Why would someone build a cabin in the middle of a forest so far away from everything?*

My head swam with questions as I took a few steps toward it.

The window was nearly solid black, caked with dirt. But as I came closer, I saw footprints in the snow leading to the cabin door.

I stopped a few feet away and cupped my hand around my mouth. "Hello? Anyone in there?" I shouted.

I thought I heard something move inside the cabin. But no one appeared in the window. No one came to the door.

I shouted again. "Anyone in there? Hello!"

Silence now. A strong burst of wind sent the rake toppling to the ground.

I stepped up to the wooden door. The wood slats were rough and unpainted. I raised a fist and knocked three times. "Hello?"

I thought I heard the floor creak inside the cabin. I had a strong hunch someone was in there.

"Hello? Anyone in there?"

I moved to the window and tried to peer inside. I couldn't see anything. Too dark in there, and the glass was smeared with mud.

With a sigh, I started to back away. But then

I stopped. And stared hard at the footprints leading up to the cabin door.

"Whoa," I murmured. I bent low to see them
better.

The prints weren't made by shoes. Or human feet.

They were made by large animal paws.

# 15

I knew I shouldn't break into the cabin. But I was curious. I told you, sometimes I act first and think second.

Besides, I didn't really break in. I gave the thin wooden door a hard push—and it scraped right open.

I glanced all around. No one inside.

Pale sunlight washed in through the grimy window. I saw a narrow cot, a low wooden chair, and a small, square table.

I took a few steps into the room. Someone had been there recently. A half-eaten sandwich sat on a plate on the table next to a smashed-in can of Coke.

I turned to the cot. The bedsheet was hanging to the floor. A solid black T-shirt was balled up for a pillow. Beside it sat a black baseball cap.

I gasped when I heard footsteps outside. I'd left the cabin door open. Was someone returning?

I spun around and ran to the door. I didn't see

anyone. The door scraped shut behind me as I closed it. I ran back to the path.

I quickly glanced over my shoulder. No one appeared behind me. Perhaps it was a forest animal that I had heard.

"How totally mysterious," I muttered to myself. I wondered if Baker knew someone was living so close to his mansion in that cabin.

As I followed the path back to the house, snow began to fall, light at first, then a storm of large flakes. The wind blew the snow in all directions. I pulled my hood up high and lowered my head as I walked.

I kicked off my boots at the back door and carried them up to my room. I pulled off the parka, covered in big white flakes, and draped it over a chair. Then my whole body gave one big shiver, trying to shake the cold away.

Dad and Ira weren't around. I guessed they were still working on the roof. I hoped they were being careful. *Those slanting shingles must be totally slick and slippery in this wet snowfall,* I thought.

I had propped my easel up in the corner. I slid it into the white light from the windows and hung the heavy art paper on it.

It took me a while to get my paints in order. A few minutes later, I sat down to work. I always like to do a light chalk drawing of what I'm going to draw. It's better than just starting out with color. And it helps me nail down exactly what the painting will be.

I decided to paint the little cabin in the forest. I sketched in the square where it would stand. And then the tall trees on either side.

I pictured a snowy scene, maybe a blanket of snow piling on the cabin's flat roof. But, of course, I would fill in the snow last.

After the sketch, I began to mix the colors I wanted to use. I needed a light brown for the wood of the cabin and a darker brown for the trees beside it.

I sat on the edge of a tall stool and leaned into the painting. I always try to imagine myself in the scene I'm painting.

I started to dab on color. I added some yellow. The cabin wall was lighter than the brown I had mixed. I needed a solid gray for the sky above it. Maybe streaked with some pale white.

I forget all about time when I'm painting. It's such an intense thing for me. I really do lose myself in the scene.

I guess I'd been working for at least half an hour when the howling started.

Long, rising and falling howls like an animal wailing in anger.

The bedroom windows were shut, but the sounds burst into the room as if the creature was very nearby.

I jumped off the stool and moved to one of the

windows. Sheets of snow were blowing against the house, gust after gust. A solid powder of white covered the glass.

Struggling to see anything clearly, I peered down at the back lawn.

Nothing in view.

Another animal cry rose up in the snowy air. Again, not mournful but angry, angry enough to send a chill down my whole body.

"Aurora—is that you?" I murmured.

I grabbed my parka and pulled it over my shoulders. Then I turned and hurried out into the hall. Maybe the big dog was locked out and wanted to come in from the snow.

I half ran, half jumped down the curving stairway. "Is anyone around?" I called breathlessly. "The howls outside—"

I didn't hear anyone.

I burst into the kitchen, heading to the back door.

"Hey—!" I let out a sharp cry as I stumbled over something big on the floor. I landed hard on my knees and spun around.

Aurora. Sprawled on his side on the kitchen floor. The big dog raised his head and yawned.

Breathing hard, I pulled myself to my feet. "So it wasn't *you* howling like that," I murmured.

I lurched toward the kitchen door. And cried out in surprise as the door crashed open.

A dark blur thundered into the kitchen surrounded by swirls of snow.

Baker. Dressed again in black. Bent over. Charging into the house like a bull. Head down, arms hanging toward the floor. Shaking his head and growling.

*Growling.*

Still bent over, he grabbed the edge of the kitchen counter. His black wool cap was caked with snow. He gave one last snarl, shaking himself, sending snowflakes flying in all directions.

Then he stood up straight—and saw me.

His eyes went wide. "Judy," he said, studying me, "how's it going? Everything okay?"

# 16

"These spring snowstorms. Always a surprise," he said. His voice was still gravelly and growly. He pulled off the wool cap and tossed it into the sink.

"I-I heard something," I stammered. "Outside."

Baker swept his hair back with both hands. His dark eyes continued to study me.

"I thought I heard Aurora," I said, then pointed. "But there he is, asleep on the floor."

Baker nodded but didn't reply.

"Did you hear the howls?" I asked.

He shook his head. "I didn't hear anything."

"Like right behind the house," I said. "Very loud. Like a wolf howling, or some other kind of animal."

Baker shook his head. "No. I was back there, Judy. I didn't hear a thing. Are you sure it wasn't the wind?"

"Pretty sure," I said.

*Pretty sure it was YOU*, I thought.

He swept back his spiky, white hair again. "Is your dad still working on the roof? I hope not. He is so stubborn. He'll never quit in the middle of a job."

Hilda entered the kitchen. "We should tell him to come down," she said. "Doesn't he have any common sense? It's too dangerous to be up there in a snowstorm."

Hilda raised a stack of brown envelopes. "But first . . . I've been looking for you, Baker," she said. "I need you to come with me. I need to show you something."

Stepping around Aurora, he started to follow her out of the kitchen. But he turned at the doorway and flashed me one last look.

"Judy, I hope you can relax here," he said. "No more howls and wild animals running around the backyard, okay? Tell your imagination to take a rest."

# 17

*I've got to talk to Dad*, I decided.

Ira said Dad had made up the story about the Beast. But I was sure that had been Baker in the backyard howling like an angry animal.

I had to tell Dad about that. And I had to tell him about the cabin in the woods.

I really wanted to leave this place. It just wasn't safe. Besides, it appeared this winter was not over yet. The snow kept coming down. If we stayed, we could get trapped up here.

I pulled up the hood on my parka and stepped outside. The snow had slowed a little, but was still coming down heavy and thick.

I couldn't believe Dad and Ira were working on the roof. Hilda was right. He has no common sense. He could finish the job when the storm passed.

I had been in such a hurry. I left my boots up in my room. The snow wasn't that deep, but my shoes kept slipping and sliding as I made my way onto the back lawn.

I turned to the house and shielded my eyes with one hand against the snow and the glare. I had to crane my neck to see up to the roof. The enormous mansion was three tall stories high.

The dark shingles slanted down steeply against the gray-white, snow-filled sky. I brushed flakes from my eyes and scanned the roof, starting with the wing on my left.

I spotted Dad near the middle of the wing, high up near the top of the roof. He sat with his legs sprawled out like a V. I saw a stack of shingles between his legs.

I didn't see Ira. Had he gone inside? Or was he on the other side of the roof?

"Hey, Dad—!" I shouted. But my voice was pushed back at me by a gust of wind.

I cupped my hand around my mouth and shouted up to him again. "Dad? Dad?" Then I waved both arms wildly above my head.

He didn't see me. He leaned forward and began to hammer a shingle.

I spotted a tall ladder tilted at the back of the house. "Okay, Dad. Here I come," I muttered.

My plan was to climb to the top of the ladder, then shout for Dad to come down. You can bet I had no plan to climb onto the roof. No way I'd let go of the ladder sides.

The climb turned out to be harder than I thought.

The metal rungs were slippery, and my shoes kept losing their grip. Wind gusts made the ladder tremble. I held the sides so tightly, my hands ached.

*What made me think this was a good idea?*

I was halfway up. The ground appeared miles below. I scolded myself for looking down.

The ladder trembled beneath me. But I figured I was too far to retreat and back down now.

"Oh." One hand slipped off the side, and I nearly toppled off. I grabbed both sides even tighter and waited for my breathing to return to normal.

Finally . . . finally, my head poked over the side of the roof. Clutching the ladder firmly, I spotted Dad leaning forward, his hammer raised.

"Hey, Dad—!" I shouted. "Dad!"

He uttered a cry. The hammer flew from his hand.

I saw his eyes go wide. His hands shot straight up in the air as he started to slide.

"Nooooooo!" A shrill scream burst from my open mouth as I watched him slip down the slanting shingles.

*I scared him. Oh no. I scared him.*

It took only seconds for him to slide to the edge of the roof. And then as I watched in breathless horror, he sailed over the edge.

Frozen in horror, I gripped the ladder—and heard him scream all the way down.

# 18

"Your dad is a very lucky man," the doctor said to Ira and me. He clicked his medical bag shut and turned away from the bed to talk to us.

Behind him, Dad slept peacefully, his hands at his sides over the blanket. After bandaging his broken ankle, the doctor gave him a shot to make him sleep.

Dr. Enright was young, with wavy blond hair and eyes as blue and shiny as marbles. He was dressed in a red-and-blue ski sweater pulled down over white ski pants.

I thought he looked more like a model or a TV actor than a doctor. But he was serious and calm and took charge immediately.

It was the first time he had been to the Grendels' house. When he arrived, he said how surprised he was that someone could build a house this size at the top of a mountain.

The doctor said that normally, he wouldn't have been nearby. But he and his wife had come

64

up to explore the mountain, thinking the winter snows were over.

"If those thick bushes along the back of the house hadn't stopped his fall," he told us, "your father probably wouldn't have survived."

In the bed behind him, Dad started to snore softly.

"He has a slight concussion," Dr. Enright said. "It gave him a pretty bad headache. That's why I gave him the shot. He needs bed rest. And, of course, I don't have X-ray equipment here. But I think his ankle is definitely broken. It isn't just a sprain."

He pointed to the crutches leaning against the wall. "When he is up and about, he shouldn't put any weight on the ankle. When he feels stronger, you'll need to get him to a hospital to have the bone set."

The doctor followed Hilda and Baker downstairs. A short while later, I heard the front door close behind him.

I took one last glance at Dad, still sleeping peacefully. Then I wandered down the long hall till I found an empty bedroom where no one would look for me. I had to be alone.

I dropped down onto the edge of the bed. Then I buried my face in my hands and started to cry.

I'm not the crying type. I almost never lose it and let the tears fall. I didn't cry when our parents split up. And I only cried a little when Flash, our dog, died last winter.

But now I couldn't help myself. I felt miserable. Devastated. Horribly guilty.

Dad had almost died, and it was all my fault.

Sob after sob escaped my throat, and my shoulders heaved up and down. My face was damp from my hot tears.

I jumped when I felt a hand on my shoulder. I raised my head to see Ira gazing down at me. "Don't cry," he said. "Dad will be okay."

He lowered himself beside me.

I rubbed the tears from my eyes with the palms of my hands. "It's . . . it's all my fault," I choked out.

"No, you can't blame yourself," Ira said softly. "Dad slipped. That wasn't your fault."

"He slipped because I startled him," I said. I pushed back my hair. It was wet from my tears. "He didn't want me to come, and he was right. I . . . I've ruined everything."

"Yes, you've ruined everything," Ira said. He chuckled.

My brother knows how to pull me from a dark mood—make fun of me.

I punched him in the side. He grabbed my fist in both hands and shoved it away.

"Why on earth did you go up to the roof?" he asked.

"To tell Dad we had to leave," I said.

"We can't leave," Ira said. "Not until Dad's

work is finished. Did you honestly think he would agree?"

"It's too scary here," I said. "I don't want to be trapped up here if there are more spring snowstorms. Baker . . . he—he scares me," I answered. "Doesn't he scare *you*, Ira?"

"He's strange, that's all," Ira replied. He jumped to his feet and stood in front of me. "But he doesn't scare me. Okay, he's big and he's loud, and he's kind of rough, but—"

"Kind of *rough*?" I cried. "Ira, I heard him out back howling like a wild animal. When he came into the house, he was growling."

Ira chuckled again. "He was probably coughing, Judy. Not growling. You have this whole Beast thing on the brain and—"

"I know. You said Dad made the Beast thing up. But I don't believe you, Ira. All the howls. All the snarls and growls."

"Listen to me—" he started.

"No. You listen to me," I said. "How dangerous is this creature? Why won't you tell me the truth about it? How scared should I be? Tell me, Ira. Just go ahead and tell me."

He shook his head. "You don't know what you're saying. You've got to stop—"

I jumped to my feet. I grabbed the front of Ira's sweater with both hands. "Baker isn't frightening," I said. "He's *terrifying*. Know what he said

67

to me? He told me to stop imagining things. But I'm *not* imagining anything. It's all *real*!"

Ira blinked several times. I could see he was thinking hard. Was he finally going to take me seriously?

Ira pulled my hands off his sweater. "Judy, I'm sure he just wanted you to calm down. And he's right. Stop being such a scaredy-cat."

I gritted my teeth and growled at my brother. "Scaredy-cat? Me? You're wrong and you know it. Why are you making excuses for Baker?"

Ira sighed and tossed his hands above his head. "I give up. See you later. Try to get it together, okay?" He stomped out of the room.

I sat there for a while on the bed in the empty room, hunched over, my hands clasped tightly in my lap. "Get it together," I muttered. "How can I get it together?"

With a sigh, I stood up and made my way back to Dad's room. He was still sleeping quietly. Then I crossed the hall to my room.

I stopped in the doorway and gazed to the windows. Staring at the easel, I let out a sharp cry.

"Oh noooo!"

My painting. My painting of the little cabin in the forest.

Someone had taken red paint—and slashed a thick red X over the whole thing.

# 19

My heart pounding, I crossed the room and stood on trembling legs in front of the easel.

I pressed my pointer finger against a line of the red X. The paint was still sticky wet.

*Who would do this?*

*Who?*

I stared at the X scrawled over the painting until it became a red blur before my eyes.

I knew what this was. It was a warning.

Someone was trying to scare me. Someone telling me to stay away from that cabin.

Whoever it was didn't know me that well. Because I don't like threats.

And now, I was more curious about the cabin than before.

I stared at the red X over my painting for another long moment. Then I spun around and ran back out into the hall. I opened my mouth to shout for Ira. But I realized I might wake Dad. So I ran down the hall to Ira's room.

"Ira?"

Not there.

"Ira? Where are you?"

I turned to the steps. Did he go down? Was he with Hilda or Baker?

I tore down the stairs, running blindly, the red X burning in my eyes. The red X shining, bright as . . . fresh blood.

"Hey, Ira?"

I found Hilda in the kitchen. She was pouring dog food into a bowl for Aurora. The dog hadn't moved from its spot in the middle of the kitchen floor.

Hilda turned to me. "Judy, you look upset," she said.

"Yes," I replied breathlessly. "I-I-my painting. In my room. Do you know anything—"

She held the bowl between her hands. "Did you do a painting? I heard you were an artist," she said. "Can I see it?"

Aurora lumbered to his feet, his eyes on the bowl.

"Uh . . . maybe later," I stammered. Hilda didn't know anything about it. "I have to see your husband," I said. I turned and hurried from the kitchen.

"You'd better not bother him. I think Baker is working," Hilda called after me.

I didn't care. I had to see him right away. Someone had destroyed my artwork. Someone in this house wanted to scare me.

I trotted through the front room into Baker's private hallway. I saw closed doors all the way down the hall.

I had only gone a few feet when Harvard stepped in front of me.

I gasped. "You scared me. Where did you come from?"

"Sorry," he said. "I have a bad habit of sneaking up on people." His pale bald head shone under the ceiling lights. He adjusted his suit jacket. "Where are you going?"

"I need to speak to Mr. Grendel right away," I said.

His face drooped. "I'm so sorry. He can't be disturbed while he's working."

I gazed down the long hall. I wondered how hard it would be to slip past Harvard and run to where Baker was working.

"Working?" I said. "You know, I asked you before. What kind of work does Mr. Grendel do?"

Harvard lowered his gaze. "I'm sorry, miss. But that's private."

I frowned at him. "You're joking, right? You really can't tell me what he does?"

"No one is allowed to know," the servant replied, avoiding my gaze.

"WHOOOOOOOAAAAAAAGH!"

A howl burst from down the hall. A shrill howl of pain that rang off the walls. Followed by another terrifying cry.

71

"That's inside the house!" I cried.

I didn't think or hesitate. I shoved Harvard with both hands. He was surprisingly light. He bounced against the wall. I took off running toward the horrible cries.

"Hey, stop!"

I ignored the servant's shout and raced down the hall.

I stopped when a door swung open a few feet ahead of me. Baker stumbled out into the hall, eyes blazing, hair wild around his red face.

"I heard cries—" I started. Then I stopped. And stared.

Were those bloodstains across the front of his white smock?

How did he get that deep, bleeding scratch across his forehead?

And then I gasped when I glanced behind him—and saw the object in a wastebasket near his desk.

A paintbrush.

Caked with red paint.

# 20

"And then what happened?" Ira asked.

"I saw the paintbrush behind him in his office," I replied. "I know I did. But I was too shocked to ask him about it. And he didn't give me a chance."

Ira squinted at me. "What do you mean?"

"Baker said he cut himself on a cabinet door, and he couldn't talk to me," I answered. "Before I could say anything else, he ran off holding his forehead."

Ira shook his head. "Weird."

It was later that night, and we were playing a game of gin rummy with a deck of cards Ira had brought. We sat on the worn carpet in his room at the side of the dark-quilted bed.

Outside the window, the sky was solid black. No moonlight or stars to brighten it even to gray. The old windowpanes rattled in the gusts of wind.

"Baker is more than weird," I said, staring at my cards. "He's frightening. And for some reason, he thinks he needs to frighten me."

Ira set his cards down on the floor. "Gin."

"You win again," I said, yawning. "One more?"

He nodded and reached to collect the cards.

"And you've been acting weird, too," I said. "I can never find you. You keep disappearing, and I know you're not working with Dad the whole time. Ira . . . I think you're keeping something from me."

His eyes grew wide. "Don't start, Judy," he said. "I'm not hiding anything from you. Seriously."

I shrugged. "Guess not. Guess I'm just stressed out." I startled as a strong wind gust made the windowpanes bang again.

Ira pressed the deck of cards into my hand. "Your deal."

We played in silence for a while. Then I sighed. "Dad says he's seeing double. And he can't put any weight on his ankle, even with the crutches the doctor gave him."

Ira frowned. "You shouldn't have come, Judy. I think we're going to be stuck here a long time. We can't move Dad. And he'll want me to finish as much of the work as I can. We really need the money."

From downstairs came the thunderous sounds of Aurora barking his head off.

I lowered my cards to my lap and listened. "Even the dog is creepy," I said. "He's as big as a horse!"

Ira snickered. "A real monster. He's definitely a good watchdog."

"But why does Baker need a watchdog?" I said. "Who is going to climb all the way up the mountain to rob his house?"

Ira didn't answer.

"Seriously," I said. "Why do you think he needs a watchdog?"

"I said he was a good watchdog. I didn't say he *needed* a watchdog," Ira replied. "Baker is a big man. He says he just likes to have a big dog."

The angry barking suddenly stopped. Ira reached for a card. "Aurora probably just saw a mouse downstairs."

"I have to tell you something," I said. "When I saw Aurora chasing a rabbit outside last night, I . . . thought he was the Beast."

"Judy, I told you—there is no Beast!" he snapped. "Give me a break, okay? Stop talking about it."

"Sorry," I muttered. I took a card from the pile. "I'll never mention it again. Promise."

Ha. If you know me, you know it was a promise I never planned to keep.

If Ira wouldn't help me, I'd find out the truth about the Beast on my own.

# 21

"Gin. We both won two games," I said. I set down my cards.

Ira climbed to his feet. "I can't believe back in the day, card games were the only thing people had for fun."

"I used to know a card trick," I said. "Maybe I can remember how to do it."

"Big whoop," Ira muttered.

"Forget it." I stood up and handed him the deck of cards. Then I turned to go to my room.

But I stopped at the doorway and turned back to him. "So . . . who do you think ruined my painting of that cabin?"

He shrugged. "Beats me. I told you I don't have a clue. It just doesn't make any sense." Then he quickly added, "I know it wasn't me."

"It shouldn't be hard to figure out," I said. "It wasn't Dad, right? That only leaves Baker and Hilda."

"Don't forget the servant dude," Ira said.

"Harvard. He's always prowling around the place. My guess would be Harvard."

"He's so creepy and weird," I said. "I told you . . . we were in the kitchen this morning, and he cut himself with a knife. And he didn't bleed. Not a drop."

Ira frowned at me. "Stop it, Judy," he said. "What are you saying? That Harvard is a zombie? You've got to stop. Zombies? Beasts? You're being ridiculous now! Maybe you should stop watching those horror films on Netflix."

I gritted my teeth. "I know what I saw."

Ira snickered. "Maybe Harvard is just anemic."

I rolled my eyes. "Yeah. For sure. Tell me this. Why would Harvard paint the red X over my painting?" I demanded. "That doesn't make any sense. I just don't get it."

Ira snickered. "I guess maybe he isn't an art lover."

"You're not funny!" I snapped. "It isn't a joke, Ira. I think someone really wants to scare me."

Ira pulled a pair of pajamas from a dresser drawer. "Maybe Dad has some ideas," he said. "If he's better tomorrow, you should definitely tell him about it."

I made my way down the hall to my room. The painting with the red X across it still stood on the easel next to the windows. I turned it around so I couldn't see it.

It took a long time to fall asleep.

*　　*　　*

The next morning, I rushed across the hall into Dad's room. He was awake and sitting up in bed. He had a mug of coffee in his hands. "Dad—how do you feel?" I cried.

A broad smile formed between his walrus mustache. "Well . . . I'm alive," he said. "Alive, but still fuzzy."

I sat down on the edge of the bed, careful not to bump the cast on his ankle. "Fuzzy?"

He blinked at me a few times. "I know there's only one of you. But I'm seeing two. Two Judys."

"You're still seeing double?"

He groaned and slid the ankle a few inches under the covers. "I guess it will take time. Luckily, I've got a hard head. It can survive any bump."

A cry escaped my throat. "Oh, Dad—I'm so sorry!" I said. I threw my arms around his shoulders and hugged him.

He waited for me to calm down. "It's okay. Really, it's okay," he said softly. "It wasn't your fault, Judy. You can't blame yourself."

"Of *course* it was my fault," I replied. "If I—"

He stopped me. "It was *my* fault," he said. "I had a harness up there. I brought it up to the roof, but I didn't strap it on. My own carelessness."

"But I—"

He raised a hand to stop me. "Enough." He took a long sip of coffee. "I'm going to be okay.

A slight concussion and a broken ankle is a small price to pay for a fall like that."

Ira appeared in the doorway. "Good morning, Dad. Judy, can I see you for a moment?"

I hurried over to him. "Dad says he is still fuzzy," I whispered. "He's seeing double."

Ira nodded. "So maybe you shouldn't tell him about what happened to your painting yet," he whispered. "We probably shouldn't upset him until he's feeling stronger."

I nodded. "You're right."

We both returned to Dad's bedside to chat for a while. "I'll be back on my feet soon," Dad said.

"You mean, back on your *foot* soon!" I joked.

Dad laughed. "In the meantime, Ira, you can do a few of the easy carpenter chores for me."

"No problem," Ira told him. "I brought a lot of Band-Aids. So I should be able to hammer away like a pro."

We all laughed. It was nice to lighten up, at least for a few minutes.

We talked a little while longer. "I have some audiobooks on my phone," I told Dad. "I'll come back after breakfast, and maybe we can listen to something."

"Meet you downstairs," Ira said to me. He disappeared out the door.

I waved good-bye to Dad and crossed the hall to my room.

"Oh!"

I stopped at my bedroom doorway and let out a startled gasp when I saw a tall guy next to the window.

"Who *are* you?" I screamed. "What are you *doing* in here?"

# 22

He spun toward me, and his eyes bulged with surprise.

He was at least sixteen or seventeen, very tall and thin. I gaped at what he was wearing. He had a black T-shirt pulled down over black jeans. And a black cap tilted over his face.

A black baseball cap.

Was it the cap I had seen in the cabin?

He motioned with both hands for me not to scream. He raised a finger to his lips.

"Wh-who are you?" I stammered. I pressed my hands against the sides of the doorway. My legs suddenly felt shaky, and I couldn't keep my heart from racing.

"Shhh." He kept his finger to his lips and took a step away from the window. He studied me as he moved closer.

"I'm calling Baker. Why are you in my room?" I cried in a shrill burst of words.

Again, he motioned with both hands for me to calm down.

But why should I calm down?

*"Answer me!"* I shrieked. "Who *are* you?"

"Nobody," he answered finally. "I'm nobody, hear?" He spoke slowly, in a deep voice. "I got turned around, that's all. No big deal."

He crept closer, arms stiffly at his sides now. His eyes locked on me and didn't blink.

"You didn't see me," he replied in his low voice from deep in his chest.

"Excuse me?" I gasped.

"You didn't see me. I didn't touch anything. I wasn't here." He pulled the black cap lower over his head "Understand? I wasn't here."

"N-no," I stammered. "I don't. Tell me. Were you in the cabin in the woods? Tell me!"

I cried out as he opened his mouth in a fierce howl, spread his arms out at his sides—and leaped at me!

# 23

"Hey—!"

I ducked to one side, but I couldn't get out of his way in time. He shoved me hard with both hands and sent me stumbling back into the hall.

His eyes were wild and another animal howl escaped his throat.

Before I could catch my balance, he swept past me and went racing down the hallway. With his long legs, he reached the stairway in seconds, and I heard him thudding down the steps.

Stunned, I shook off my fear and took off after him. He was already out of sight by the time I reached the stairs. But I spun down the curving staircase as fast as I could.

I heard running footsteps in the front room. I took a deep, shuddering breath and followed the sounds. No one in the living room.

I made my way through the heavy, dark furniture. The stern faces on the wall portraits passed by in a blur.

The sound of the footsteps was muffled, distant now. But I followed the long hall, trotting breathlessly.

When I neared the den, a loud growl made me stop.

I was panting hard, and I could feel hot drops of sweat on my cheeks and forehead.

I cupped my hands around my ears and listened. I heard angry snarls, low growls, heavy thuds, and bangs.

"Oh." I heard a human groan. And then more animal sounds. Another groan.

I froze for a moment, my hands still at my ears. My whole body shuddered.

*What is going on in there?*

I had to know. I forced my legs to move. I stumbled into the den—and let out a cry of surprise.

I stared at Baker, on all fours, down on the carpet. He had his arms around Aurora's back, as if tackling him. It took me a few seconds to realize they were wrestling.

Growling and snapping at each other, both of them snarling and groaning, they rolled over one another. Baker finally stopped when he saw me standing there watching.

He let go of his grip on the big dog and raised himself onto his elbows. A smile spread over his face. "Judy—"

"I-I—" My words caught in my throat.

"Aurora and I were having a little playtime," Baker said. He twisted himself into a sitting position. He dusted off the front of his shirt with both hands.

Aurora didn't want to quit. He bumped Baker from behind, then licked the back of Baker's neck.

Baker gently pushed the dog's big head away. His smile faded as he saw the distressed look on my face. "Judy? What's wrong?"

"There . . . was a boy in my room," I stammered.

Baker blinked. "Say again?"

"A boy. In my room," I told him. "Dressed in black. With a black baseball cap. I caught him. In my room. A stranger."

Baker narrowed his eyes at me. "Come on, Judy," he said with a groan, "you've got to relax. Are you talking about the electrician who came to inspect the circuit breakers?"

My mouth dropped open. I couldn't speak. "Electrician?" I finally choked out.

He nodded. "A young fellow," he said. "Came to check out the breakers on your floor."

I wanted to scream at the top of my lungs: "I don't believe you. Why would an electrician shove me out of the way and run down the stairs?"

I knew he had to be lying. But how could I argue with him?

I let out a choked gasp, turned, and strode out of the room.

*No more,* I told myself. *I don't have time for Baker's lies. I've had it. I'm fed up with everybody being so mysterious.*

I knew what I saw. I saw the boy dressed in black in my room. He wasn't an electrician. Where were his tools? He warned me not to tell anyone. He shoved me out of the way and took off.

I ran back through the empty living room, my angry thoughts boiling and bubbling. I knew what I was going to do. I was going to learn the truth. Get to the bottom of things. Find out why everyone in the Grendels' house was acting so strange.

"I'll search everywhere till I find that boy," I told myself. "I'll find the boy—and the Beast—and put an end to all these lies."

# 24

Once again, my head felt about to burst. But at least I knew I couldn't rely on anyone else. I had to solve the mystery of this place on my own.

I needed fresh air. I had to get out of the house and clear my head.

I was returning to my room to get my parka and boots. But the sad-eyed servant Harvard stepped in front of me before I got to the stairway.

"Can I help you, Miss Judy?" he asked.

I tried to scoot past him, but he didn't budge. "No, you can't," I snapped.

His eyes went wide with surprise. "If there's anything I can do . . ." His voice trailed off.

"You know you can't help me," I shouted. "You know you won't tell me the truth about anything." My angry outburst surprised even me.

He swallowed noisily and took a few steps back. He lowered his gaze to the floor. "I'm sorry if I did something to offend you," he muttered.

I darted around him and leaped onto the stairway. He watched me race up the stairs.

*He's useless,* I thought. *He won't even tell me what Baker's work is.*

I reached the second floor and hurried to Ira's room. Empty.

Where was he? Why wasn't he ever in his room when I needed him?

I wanted to tell him about the boy in my room. I wanted Ira to come out for a walk with me so we could talk. Ira was the only one I could talk to.

"Ira?" I called his name even though he wasn't there.

Then I remembered. Dad had given him some simple carpentry jobs to do. Ira was somewhere in this giant house making repairs.

I made my way down the hall and checked in on Dad. Hilda was just taking away his breakfast tray. "Your dad is doing much better." She pointed to his coffee mug. "That's his third cup. We don't want him to get *too* wired—do we?"

"I can handle it," Dad called from the bed.

I took Hilda's arm before she walked to the door. "Is anyone else staying here?" I asked.

She squinted at me and didn't reply.

"Maybe you can help me," I said. "There was a boy in my room. A teenager. Dressed all in black. Do you know who he is?"

She shook her head.

"Is anyone else in the house?" I demanded. "Anyone else staying here or visiting here? An electrician?"

"Judy, I don't know anything about that," Hilda said. "You'll have to ask Baker about that."

"You don't know who I mean?" I demanded.

She shook her head again. "I don't know. I really don't."

Still holding her by the arm, I studied her face. Was she lying?

I stared into her eyes. I couldn't tell.

"Sorry," I muttered. I'm not sure why I thought I should apologize. I let go of her arm.

She strode to the door with the tray between her hands. "Have a nice afternoon, Judy," she said as she disappeared into the hall.

"What was *that* about?" Dad asked.

"Nothing," I said. "I thought I saw someone."

I didn't want to trouble Dad. "How are your eyes?" I asked.

He sighed. "I don't feel like myself yet. Sorry to say it. And I'm still seeing double. Guess it will take time."

I glanced out the window. "The snow seems to have stopped," I said. "I think I'm going to take a walk."

"Come see me again when you get back," Dad said. "And don't go too far, okay?"

I was desperate to tell Dad about the red X

splashed over my painting and about the guy I caught in my room. But I could see he was still fuzzy-minded, still not himself.

I promised I'd be back soon. Then I crossed the hall to my room.

I pulled my parka from the closet and slid into it. I shoved the wool gloves I'd brought into the pockets.

*Where's my phone?* I couldn't text or make calls up here. But I could take photos, and I wanted to take some pictures of the little cabin. I wanted to go back to that cabin and get proof.

"Where *are* you, phone?" I said aloud, this time glancing at the bed table. I didn't see it at first.

Then I did. "Oh no."

I saw the metal frame on the bed table. And some pieces on the floor. And the panel of glass, cracked and shattered.

"Oh no. Oh noooo."

I stared at my phone—smashed to bits.

# SLAPPY HERE, EVERYONE.

Don't you hate it when someone smashes your phone? That could spoil your whole day! Haha.

I'm beginning to think maybe there *is* a beast in Baker Grendel's house.

Do you know the best way to deal with a beast? Long distance! Hahaha.

I think Judy better borrow her dad's phone and text: *H-E-L-P! Get me out of this story!*

# 25

I picked up the broken phone with a trembling hand. The glass was totally shattered. Jagged pieces fell off in my palm.

My glance fell on a yellow scrap of paper that had been under the phone. I bent to read it. Scrawled in red ink it said, *A warning. Stop asking questions. You won't like the answers.*

I gasped. The paper fell from my hand.

I couldn't take this anymore. I couldn't deal with this. I had no choice.

Gripping the shattered phone in my hand, I bolted across the hall into Dad's room. "Look at this! *Look* at this!" I wailed.

A book fell from his hands as he turned to me in surprise. "Judy—what—?"

I shoved the phone in his face. "My phone! Someone did this, Dad. Someone smashed it!" I cried.

He squinted at it. His cheeks turned bright pink. "I don't understand. I don't—"

"Someone left a note. On my bed table," I said, lowering the phone to my side. "It said it was a warning. It said not to ask questions."

"But who—?" The circles on Dad's cheeks darkened to purple.

I knew he wasn't feeling well. I knew he was still weak and seeing double. But I had no choice. I needed help.

My voice shrill and breathless, I let it all out. I told him everything in one breathless burst of words.

"I found a little cabin hidden by trees in the forest. It looked like someone was living there, but I didn't see anyone. I started a painting of it in my room, and someone ruined it. Someone painted a red X over my painting."

Dad pulled himself up in the bed. His mouth hung open as he listened to my story.

"This morning, I caught a boy in my room. A stranger. A teenager," I continued. "He wouldn't tell me what he was doing here. He . . . he threatened me, Dad. He said I shouldn't tell anyone I saw him."

Dad shut his eyes. He shook his head. He didn't say a word.

I couldn't stop. I had to finish my story. "I chased the boy downstairs, but I lost him. I found Baker with his dog. I told him about the boy, and . . . and he said he was just an electrician he had hired. But I know that's not true."

I tossed the broken phone into the waste-basket beside the bed. "What's going on, Dad? Tell me," I pleaded. I felt hot tears covering my eyes. "What's this all about? Who is trying to scare me?"

Dad slowly opened his eyes. He squinted at me. I guessed he was still seeing two of me. I knew he had a concussion, but I was too angry and frightened to care now. I needed answers.

He cleared his throat. I could see his mind was spinning. He was thinking hard.

"It will be okay," he said finally. He smoothed down his walrus mustache.

"Okay?" I screamed. "*Okay?* How can it be okay?"

"I will take care of it," Dad said quietly.

"What . . . what are you *talking* about?" I cried, tearing at the sides of my hair. "How can you—"

"Trust me. I will take care of it," he repeated.

"You're not making any sense!" I shouted. "How can you take care of it? You're flat on your back with a broken ankle and a concussion. Dad, you can't even see straight!"

"You'll see," he said. Then he started to cough.

His nonanswers were just making me angrier. He wasn't telling the truth. Lying there in bed, he couldn't take care of anything.

"Dad, let's go home," I said. "I'm sorry I sneaked up here. Really. But, please—take me home."

He squinted at me. I could see that his eyes

weren't right. He looked as if he was trying to remember who I was.

"I'll take care of it," he said again. "Trust me, Judy. I'll take care of everything."

I turned away and headed toward the door. "Never mind, Dad."

What was the point of arguing with him? He wasn't himself. He couldn't help me.

"Maybe I can get Ira on my side," I told myself. With his help, maybe we could at least get Dad to agree to leave this horrid place.

I zipped my parka up to the top and lowered the hood over my head. I pulled on my wool gloves and made my way to the kitchen and out the door.

A light snow was falling from a dark sky. The icy air felt good against my hot cheeks.

I took a few deep breaths. I wanted the cold, fresh air to calm me down. But my chest still felt fluttery, and I could feel the blood pulsing at my temples.

The ground was crunchy hard beneath my boots as I started to walk. Patches of snow were forming in the tall grass behind the house.

I took a few steps, then stopped. I pulled back when I saw a shadow move at the side of the house. I retreated to the bushes along the wall of the house.

Someone was walking away from the house. Taking long, quick strides.

I shielded my eyes with one hand to see better.

Baker Grendel.

Bundled in his bulging, black fur coat with a black wool ski cap pulled down over his face. Baker had his head lowered, his arms swinging at his sides. He cut through the tall grass like a steamship plowing through water.

Was he heading to the forest?

Why was he walking so quickly, in such a hurry?

I watched him till he was nearly to the back of the lawn. Then I decided I had to follow him.

# 26

I brushed snowflakes off my eyebrows. The snow was falling steadily now, large flakes falling straight down from a windless sky.

Up ahead, Baker followed the path into the trees. I held back. I didn't want him to hear my footsteps and turn around and discover me behind him.

I had to force myself to breathe. My legs felt as if they weighed a thousand pounds as I moved forward, following the path to the trees.

Why was he walking into the forest? He didn't have Aurora with him, so it wasn't a dog walk.

The tall trees formed a thick canopy overhead. It made it seem as if the snow had stopped. But the trees also kept the light out, and as I moved deeper into the forest, it became nearly as dark as night.

Was Baker still up ahead? The path had turned, and I didn't see him.

A sudden thought made me gasp. What if he

turned around and started to walk back? He would walk right into me.

I had to know where he was going. But I didn't want to walk off the path. In the dim light, it would be so easy to get lost.

I followed the curve of the path and squinted into the distance. I couldn't see Baker anywhere.

My boots slid over a carpet of dead leaves on the hard dirt. A tree had fallen across the path. I climbed over it and found myself in a small clearing.

No sign of Baker up ahead. Did I give him too much of a head start?

I paused to catch my breath. My gaze traveled over a clump of tall reeds and some scraggly shrubs at the edge of the clearing.

And then I saw it.

I bit my lips to keep from screaming.

I gaped at the tall creature stepping out from the trees. Its face hidden in folds of black fur. Its thick body wrapped in fur.

An animal?

Could it be? No. It was at least eight feet tall. It walked on two legs with heavy, pounding footsteps. Two legs like a human.

But it wasn't human. Its head bobbed up and down with every thudding footstep. It turned toward me, and I stifled another scream as I saw its face.

A human face!

A human face surrounded by black animal fur. The head bobbing, the fur-covered chest heaving in and out as it strode into the clearing.

Not a human. Not an animal.

The Beast!

A real beast. It existed. It was real!

Back home, Dad had told the truth. And since we arrived here, everyone had lied to me.

Baker. He had to be the Beast.

Of *course*, he was the Beast.

He walked out to the forest to become the Beast. I *knew* it!

My hand still pressed against my mouth, I stared at him, my whole body shuddering, my legs rubbery, ready to collapse.

A frightening animal walking upright like a human. But wrapped in fur. And with front paws like bear claws! A human face and claws like a bear.

Oh no. Was that *me* whistling?

Yes. I couldn't hold it in. I was whistling, as I always did when I was afraid.

The creature turned.

It stared at me with pale, human eyes. It frowned. Its human mouth uttered a low growl.

And now it leaned its big body forward. Stuck out its bearlike paws. And with another, louder growl, showed its teeth and came charging at me.

# 27

I spun around. Fell. Hit the hard ground on my elbows and knees.

Pain shot up and down my body.

The animal growls rang out close behind me.

Gasping for breath, I pulled myself up and took off running. My boots slid on the slippery dead leaves. I leaned into the wind like a sprint runner and ran blindly—the trees, the shrubs, the tall grass shooting past in a gray blur.

I glanced back. The ugly creature was closing in on me, snarling. Thick drool poured from its open jaws. Its paws groped the air, ready to grab me. Its deep-throated, angry growls sent cold chills down my back.

I lurched forward, running desperately.

*Baker, I know it's you.*

*Baker, why are you chasing me? Do you really plan to hurt me? Hurt me because I know your secret?*

Up ahead, I spotted a large slab of rock in the

path. I leaped over it and turned into the tall grass and weeds along the side.

The heavy *thud* of the Beast's hind paws on the dirt pounded in my ears.

Everything grew even darker as I ran from the path, into a deep tangle of trees.

The Beast wheezed with every breath as it came after me. It was panting noisily, but it didn't slow down.

I saw two fat tree trunks tangled around each other up ahead. I ducked around them and pressed myself tightly against the cold, rough bark.

I tried to press myself into the tree. Make myself invisible behind these wide trunks.

Did he see me?

Could he smell me? Sense where I was?

I ignored the sharp, throbbing pain in my side and struggled to hold my breath.

Silence. Silence now.

I shifted my weight. Carefully poked my head out from the thick trunk to take a peek.

A hard claw gripped my ankle tightly from behind—and I screamed.

# 28

I slammed against the tree trunk. Panic froze my whole body.

I glanced down. No. Oh, wait. Not a claw.

The Beast hadn't grabbed my ankle. I had stepped into a forked twig that had fallen from the tree.

Peeking out, I saw the Beast turn. He had lost me. But my scream drew him back.

I hugged the tree trunk as he came lumbering toward me.

I took a deep breath and forced myself to move. Pushed myself away from the safety of the trunk and ran. The chase was on again.

When we were little, Ira and I used to play a running game of tag. Walking wasn't allowed. We ran at each other, and we tagged each other with a hard slap. We called it Slap Tag.

It flashed into my mind as I ran through the trees, chased by this growling man-beast. But I knew if I was caught, the game wouldn't end in just a slap.

I leaped over a fallen branch and turned sharply into a thicket of evergreen shrubs. To my surprise, the thundering footsteps behind me slowed.

I whipped around and saw the creature had become tangled in hanging vines. They wrapped around his shoulders like snakes. He battled them, swiping at them, snarling furiously.

I ducked down low behind the shrubs. I suddenly realized I was whistling. Whistling loudly.

The Beast stopped swiping at the vines. He tilted his head. He must have heard my whistles. He raised his front paws and pressed them against his ears. He uttered a painful howl.

I could see that he couldn't stand my whistling. The sound seemed to paralyze him!

Now was my chance to put some distance between us.

I spun away from the bushes—and saw the square cabin up ahead across a small clearing.

*I can hide inside. Maybe he won't see me. Maybe he'll lose me again.*

I forced my legs to move. Slipping over the dead leaves and low weeds, I ran full speed. I could hear the Beast's angry grunts as he battled free of the vines. But I didn't turn around to see if he was coming after me again.

My heart pounding, my throat aching and dry, my legs throbbed with each running stride . . .

I slammed up against the cabin door. My hand shook as I grabbed the rusted door knob. I pulled hard and the door scraped open.

And I stared at a boy standing against the wall.

"Wh-who *are* you?" I choked out.

"Get out!" he shouted. "Get out! Go away! *Now!*"

# 29

"No. No. Please," I said. I stepped into the cabin. I shut the door behind me and pressed my back against it.

"You can't be here!" he cried. "You can't see me."

He was at least fifteen or sixteen, but shorter than me. I'd never seen him before. He wasn't the boy in black I had caught in my room.

He had straight blond hair over a round face, dark eyes that were wide with surprise. He wore a baggy maroon sweatshirt over dark jeans. "I . . . I have to hide," I explained. I could hear the growls of the Beast through the door.

"You can't be here," the boy said. He didn't move from against the wall. "It isn't right."

"*What?*" I cried. "What do you mean?"

For the first time, I realized he was *afraid*.

"You're not supposed to see me," he said again. "Go away. Please. Get out. Before . . . before something bad happens."

"Something bad?" I cried. "Like what?"

Before he could answer, I heard the loud *thuds* of the Beast's heavy footsteps. Heard the creature's wheezing breaths, right outside the cabin. Close. Very close. On the other side of the door.

I held my breath and pressed my back hard against the door. I raised a finger to my lips. "Shhhhh," I whispered. "Please . . . please don't let him hear us."

He didn't move. He stared at me, wide-eyed. His body was tensed and his fists were clenched, as if ready to fight.

I held my breath until my chest ached, listening . . . listening.

On the other side of the door, the Beast grew quiet. I could hear him circling the cabin. Once. Twice. I heard the crackle of leaves and the bump of heavy feet on the frozen dirt.

Then silence.

I didn't move.

I waited some more. Time seemed to stand still.

The boy finally moved. He narrowed his dark eyes at me and strode closer. "He's gone," he said, just above a whisper.

I took a deep breath. I listened hard. Silent out there.

"Stop it!" the boy snapped.

He startled me. "Stop what?"

"Stop that whistling," he answered.

"I . . . I didn't know I was whistling," I told him.

"Well, stop it," he said. "It hurts my ears."

"S-sorry," I stammered. "I always whistle when I'm scared. My brother hates it, too."

He studied me. "Your brother?"

I nodded. "Have you seen him? He's about your age. His name is Ira."

He didn't answer my question. "You have to go," he said. "Please go."

"Who are you?" I demanded. "Why are you in this cabin?"

He didn't answer. Instead, he moved me out of the way and pushed open the cabin door.

A rush of cold air blew in over both of us. He motioned for me to leave.

I stopped in the doorway and gazed all around. No sign of the Beast.

Had he really given up?

"Do you know that other boy?" I demanded. "The tall boy who wears the black cap?"

He didn't answer. Just stared out at the trees. Snowflakes began to fall. They fluttered and danced on the swirling gusts of wind.

I pulled my hood over my head. "Do you know him? The other boy?" I repeated my question. "Tell me. Tell me why you're here in this cabin."

"You didn't see me. You're not supposed to see me," came the same reply.

*Strange. That's what the first boy had said.*

I walked out into the snow.

I scanned the clearing and the trees on the other side to make sure the Beast had gone, and started to trot toward the path. I heard the cabin door close behind me.

Who was that boy?

And the boy I had found in my room?

There was so much I didn't know.

But I *had* cleared up one mystery. I knew now that Baker could turn into a half-human, half-animal beast. And I knew how vicious and dangerous he could be.

Dad *had* to know it. Is that why he didn't want me to come up here?

But if he *did* know the truth about Baker, why did he bring Ira here every spring? Why did Dad come at all? Did we really need the money badly enough to make it worth the risk?

The questions raced through my mind as I ran along the path toward the house. This time, I wasn't going to let Dad off the hook. This time, I was going to insist on answers.

I burst into the kitchen from the back door. Warm air surrounded me. It still smelled of bacon from breakfast.

No one there. I tugged back my hood and raced through the front rooms to the stairway. Shaking snow off the shoulders of my parka, I darted up the stairs.

"Ira? Are you up here?" I shouted down the long hallway. "Ira?"

The door to his room was closed. "Ira, are you in there?"

I shoved open the door and strode inside. "Ira?"

Not here. His bed had been made. His pajamas and the other clothes he had tossed onto the floor were gone. I checked the closet. Empty. "Ira, where are you?" I said, talking to myself.

Back in the hall, I struggled to catch my breath. Was Ira with Dad? Or was he still somewhere in the house doing carpentry work?

It was time to get some answers from Dad.

I knew he wasn't feeling exactly right. And I knew he was probably feeling very sorry for himself now. He hated to stay in bed.

But none of that mattered to me. I had to know the truth. I needed answers to all my questions.

I stepped into Dad's room. "Dad, you have to talk to me," I said. "I know—"

I stopped.

Where was he?

He wasn't in his bed. My eyes scanned the room. The crutches weren't against the wall where I had seen them last. His closet door was closed.

"Dad—?"

I heard a cough. And turned back to the door.

Harvard stepped into the room, adjusting his tie. "Hello, Miss Judy," he said. He spread his hand over his mouth and coughed again.

"Harvard, where—?" I started.

"Are you looking for your father and your brother?" he asked.

I nodded. "Yes, I am. I need to talk to my dad right away."

His sad, dark-ringed eyes locked on mine. "I'm so sorry," he said. "They left."

# 30

"No!" I cried. "They *couldn't*! They wouldn't leave without me!"

Harvard sighed. "I'm so sorry. They had to leave, Miss Judy."

"No. No. No," I kept repeating, shaking my head. "Where are they, Harvard? I know they wouldn't leave without me."

I could feel the blood pulsing at my temples. I suddenly felt cold all over. I knew he was lying. He had to be lying.

"Baker asked them to leave," Harvard said, his dark eyes watery as they gazed hard at me.

"But they wouldn't go without me!" I shrieked. "That's impossible!"

I brushed past him into the hall. I ran into Dad's room.

Yes. The crutches were gone. I pulled open his closet door. Empty. I saw a single white sock on the closet floor. Nothing else.

*No. No. No way.*

I tried the dresser against the wall. The top drawer was stuck shut. I tugged out the second drawer. Nothing inside. The bottom drawer was empty, too.

*No. No way they would leave without me.*

With a frantic cry, I ran to Ira's room. I searched everywhere. I even got down on the floor and searched under the bed.

Nothing there. No sign he was ever in the room.

My brain was spinning. I struggled to think of a reason why the two of them would leave me here. Leave me here without even saying good-bye.

I couldn't think of one.

Had Baker scared them away?

They *had* to know Baker is the Beast. Did he force them to leave me here by threatening them? Terrifying them?

I slumped back to my room. Harvard had left. I closed the door behind me and dropped onto the edge of the bed. I lowered my head to my hands, shut my eyes, and tried to think.

But the more I thought, the more my panic grew.

I knew I was in terrible danger. Alone in this house with the Beast.

Dad and Ira couldn't protect me.

*Is there anyone here who can help me?*

Hilda flashed into my mind. Would she help me get away from her husband, the Beast? Would she help me go after Ira and my Dad?

Hilda was the only person I could try.

I crossed the room and started to open the bedroom door.

The knob turned in my hand, but the door wouldn't slide open.

I tried again, turning the knob the other way and tugging harder.

No.

No.

The door was locked. Someone had locked me in.

# 31

Trapped in this frightening old mansion with the Beast!

Who locked me in this room? It had to be Harvard.

But why?

What did the Beast plan to do to me? Now that I knew Baker's secret, what did he have in mind for me?

It couldn't be anything good.

My hands were ice-cold. I clasped them in front of me and walked to the window.

I peered down to the back lawn below. I was up too high. No way I could jump or lower myself to the ground.

And if I did somehow escape the house, where would I go? There was no village or town up here. No one else who lived this high up the mountain.

I spun around when I heard a soft knock on the door.

I heard the click of keys, and then the door

scraped open. Harvard poked his bald head into the room. "Baker would like to see you now," he said.

He stood holding the doorknob, waiting for me to walk over to him.

But I crossed my arms in front of me and didn't move from the window.

"Why are you doing this?" I cried. "Why are you following his orders? Don't you know what he is?"

Harvard nodded. "I know what he is, Miss Judy. I've worked here for thirty years." He motioned for me to move.

I knew I couldn't just stand there by the wall staring at him. So I followed him out into the hall.

He gripped my arm as we started down the winding staircase.

I knew each step took me closer to my doom.

"Harvard, please," I choked out. "Won't you help me? Help me escape this place?"

He was silent for a long moment. We followed the stairway down. "I can't," he answered finally. He kept his eyes straight ahead. "We have to listen to him and obey him."

We were nearly at the bottom. A scream burst from my throat. "NOOOO!"

I jerked my arm free from his grasp—and ran.

"Come back!" His shoes thudding on the steps, Harvard came after me.

I hit the floor running. *But where should I go? Which way? Which way?*

My eyes darted from one hall to the other. Finally, I forced myself to take off, racing away from Baker's wing of the house, away from his office and dining room.

My shoes slapped against the dark carpet. The stern faces on the tall oil paintings flew past me in a dark blur.

*I've got to get out of this house,* I told myself. *It's my only chance.*

I turned a corner—and let out a scream.

The two boys appeared from out of nowhere to block my path. The boys I had seen before. They each grabbed one of my arms, holding me tightly in place.

I couldn't slow my panting breaths. I stood there for a long moment, waiting for my shock to wear off. Then I gave a hard tug backward, trying to free myself.

"Get *off* me!" I yelled. "Let me go!"

I wasn't strong enough to pull away from them. I shoved my head against the tall boy's arm and tried to bite him.

"Stop fighting!" he cried in a loud whisper. He gazed over my shoulder. Was Harvard charging toward us down the hall?

"Come with us. Hurry! We'll help you," he said.

*Should I trust them?*

I knew I didn't have a choice. They each held one of my arms as we started to run down the hall. We bumped shoulders as we ran. They swung around into another long hallway, and I had to follow.

"Where are you taking me?" I demanded.

They kept their eyes straight ahead. "Don't worry," the boy in black said. "We're helping you."

"Don't fight us," the other boy said. "You'll be okay."

Our running footsteps echoed off the walls and high ceiling. The blond guy kept falling a little behind, causing me to stumble.

"Who *are* you?" I demanded, shouting over the ringing sound of our shoes on the carpet. "Where are we going? Why are you helping me?"

They acted as if they didn't hear me. They half carried me over the floor as we ran. At the end of the hall, they suddenly stopped.

I struggled to catch my breath. We stood in front of a dark wooden door. The door had a brass nameplate on it. I squinted to read it.

BAKER GRENDEL.

The boys weren't rescuing me. They had taken me right to Baker's office.

They had taken me to my doom.

# 32

"Noooo!"

A loud gasp escaped my throat.

I turned and head-butted the blond boy in the stomach. He groaned—grabbed his belly—and stumbled into the other boy.

I tugged free, dodged away from them. And started running again.

*I'm going to run forever,* I thought. *Run back and forth through these halls. Until . . .*

Until what?

I knew I had to get out of the house. No way I could be safe until I got away from here.

I spun around a corner and kept going. I could hear Aurora barking in the distance. I saw a side entrance at the end of the hall.

Yes!

If only I could get there before they stopped me again.

I was panting hard. My legs throbbed with every running step.

I was a few feet from the door when I heard a loud *thud*. Several *thuds*.

Someone pounding on the other side of a door near the entrance.

I stopped. I struggled to catch my breath.

I stared at the closed door. And listened to the pounding.

And then a voice: "Let us out! Can you hear me? Let us out!"

"Ira!" I cried.

"Judy? Is that you?" Ira shouted.

"Judy, let me out! Hurry!" Dad called.

"I-I can't believe it!" I stammered. "You're here. He locked you in."

I dove for the door. A key was in the lock. I grabbed it with a trembling hand and twisted it.

The door burst open. Ira and my dad came rushing out. Dad was leaning on his crutches. His face was red. His eyes scanned up and down the hall.

I threw my arms around him. "Dad, why—?" I started.

He shook his head. "No time to explain. You're not safe. We—"

Ira stood stiffly, his back against the wall. His eyes were wide, and he had the strangest expression on his face.

Was it fear? Was it confusion? I couldn't tell.

"You're not safe," Dad said, glancing to the front door.

A weird sound escaped Ira's open mouth. Something between a choked cry and a gasp.

"Not safe," Dad repeated, eyes wide with alarm.

And to my surprise, he grabbed Ira by the shoulders and pushed him backward. Dad tried to push Ira back into the room.

"Dad, what are you *doing*?" I screamed.

He shoved Ira again. "Not safe," Dad repeated.

And then Ira shoved him back.

One of Dad's crutches fell to the floor. Dad stumbled against the wall.

And I saw my brother start to change.

It only took seconds. Ira's face disappeared in a thick layer of fur. Dark hair sprouted over his hands and throat.

He opened his jaws to reveal two rows of jagged fangs. He clawed the air with fur-covered animal paws.

"Oh noooo," I moaned.

Ira tossed back his head and roared. The roar echoed down the hall and rang in my ears.

And then Baker rumbled into view. His voice rose over the roar. "What have you done?" He came running toward us. "The Beast is loose! The Beast is loose!"

# 33

My brother. My brother Ira was the Beast.

I stood there openmouthed, not breathing, not moving. Staring at the half-human creature, my brother.

He swiped the air with a big paw and uttered another angry roar.

I gasped. His eyes were on me now. Did he plan to attack?

Baker ran up to us, breathing noisily. He shielded his face with both arms as the Beast swung a paw at him.

"Start whistling," Baker shouted. "Everyone— whistle! Hurry!"

I didn't understand. But I didn't hesitate. I pressed my lips together and began to whistle as loud as I could.

Dad whistled, too. And Baker joined in.

The shrill sounds rang off the walls.

Ira's beast eyes went wide. He opened his jaws

in an angry growl. But the growl grew softer, weaker before it ended.

He covered both furry ears. Pressed his paws against them. He appeared to shrink. He sank back weakly against the wall. And dropped to his knees.

We kept whistling, whistling a rising, falling sound, like a shrill siren.

Holding his ears, the Beast curled in on himself. He shut his eyes and uttered a soft howl of pain.

Ira never could stand my whistling. And now I knew why. It was because of the beast part of him. The Beast hated my whistling.

Quickly the fur on his face faded back into his skin. His hands were pale again as all the fur vanished. I couldn't take my eyes away. I didn't want to see this. I didn't want to see any of it.

But in a few seconds, I was staring at Ira's normal face, his normal body. Huddled on the floor, he curled against the wall. His eyes were shut. His mouth was drawn into a tight grimace of pain.

Baker gave a signal, and we stopped whistling. Ira's body heaved in a violent shudder.

"Judy," Dad said, "we tried to keep it from you. We tried to keep you from finding out. We didn't want you to know."

"Take Ira away," Baker ordered my dad. "Take him out to the cabin. I'll come visit him later."

Leaning on his crutches, Dad reached down and pulled Ira to his feet. Ira didn't resist. He kept his head lowered and his shoulders hunched. And he followed Dad out the door.

I hugged myself, trying to calm my racing heart. I struggled to catch my breath.

Baker watched Dad and Ira leave the house. Then he turned to me. "Come with me, Judy," he said.

I pulled back. Alone now, I didn't know what to do.

"Come with me," Baker repeated, motioning for me to follow him.

I swallowed hard and took a few steps toward him.

*Now what?*

# 34

Staying a few feet behind him, I followed Baker back down the long hall to his office. I stopped at the door, but he motioned for me to come in.

The room had a thick purple carpet and purple drapes on a window that started at the floor and rose to the ceiling.

A wide glass-topped desk stood by one wall. Across from it, two black leather chairs.

"Sit down, Judy," he said softly.

"I don't want to sit down!" I cried. "I want to get out of here. I-I don't understand—"

He motioned to the chairs with one big hand. "I'm going to explain it all. Just have a seat, okay?"

I had no choice. I dropped into one of the chairs.

He sat down heavily behind the desk and leaned toward me. "I know what you thought," he said. "You thought I was the Beast."

I opened my mouth but no words came out.

"That's okay," he said softly. "You can tell the truth."

"Well . . . y-yes," I stammered. "I thought you were the Beast."

"You have to trust me," he started. "I—"

"I *can't* trust you," I said, my voice high and shrill. "Why did you lock up my dad and Ira?"

"Because I knew you were in danger," Baker replied. "I did it for your own safety, Judy."

He swept a hand back through the tangles of his white hair. "I'm so sorry you had to learn the truth. As your dad said, we tried to keep you from finding out."

"That my brother Ira is the Beast?" I said.

He nodded.

I took a deep breath. "Ira was the beast that chased me in the woods?"

He nodded again. "Yes. I was keeping him in that cabin where I treat my patients."

"But—" I started.

He leaned closer over the desktop. "Judy, listen to me," he said softly. "Why do you think your dad brings Ira up here every spring? For me to treat. I'm the only scientist who knows how to deal with these young people who have the Beast disease, who can't help themselves . . . People who become beasts every spring."

"You? You're a *scientist*?" I said.

He nodded. He motioned to two framed documents on the wall behind him. Diplomas?

"Those two boys who brought you to my office . . . They are here for my treatment as well," he said.

"But . . . but . . . Ira . . ." I couldn't find words.

"I don't need your dad to do the carpentry work for me every spring," Baker said. "I can do it myself. It was just an excuse for him to bring Ira to see me."

"Is that why Dad never wanted me to come?" I asked.

Baker nodded again. "He did everything in his power to keep you from learning the truth about your brother."

He leaned back in the desk chair. "After my treatments each spring, it's safe for Ira to go home till the next spring."

My brain felt about to explode. A million thoughts buzzed through my head at once. I rubbed my temples, but I couldn't smooth the thoughts away.

"My painting of the cabin . . ." I choked out. "The red X across it. My phone . . . smashed to pieces . . ."

"I'm sorry," Baker murmured. "Ira did those things. He wasn't in control. He couldn't help himself."

"But I saw a paintbrush with red paint in your office," I said.

"Ira must have put it there to throw you off the track," Baker said.

I shut my eyes. I thought it might make it easier to think straight. But it didn't help.

"Harvard is another sample of my work," Baker said. "I cured him of the Beast disease. Sadly, I have to keep him anemic as part of the cure. But he manages well. He hasn't had a Beast episode in years."

Slowly, I opened my eyes and gazed at him. "Okay," I said. "Okay. I believe you. I believe you're telling me the truth."

"I'm sorry," he whispered. "It's very sad. But I *am* telling you the truth."

"I'm sorry, too," I said. "I'm sorry I thought you were the Beast. I didn't know."

He nodded but didn't reply.

I finally uncrossed my arms and let them fall to the arms of the chair. "Now that I know the truth ..." I said ... "can I go home with Dad and Ira?"

Baker sat up straight. His expression darkened. "I'm sorry," he said. "You can't."

# 35

I jumped to my feet. My hands curled into tight fists. I shook them at him.

"Why not?" I cried. "You can't keep me prisoner here. You have to let me go home."

He didn't move. "Judy, when is your thirteenth birthday?" he asked.

"It's . . . in a few days," I stammered. "But—"

He raised a hand to silence me. "Okay. You have to stay here so I can watch you."

"Why—?"

"Since your brother has the Beast disease," Baker said, "it is possible that you have it, too."

"No way—" I started.

"If you also have it," Baker said, "we would see the first signs anytime now."

"That's ridiculous!" I cried, shaking my fists again. "You have to let me go. You *have* to!"

I had both fists in the air. The sleeves of my sweater slid up.

I saw my arms—and screamed.

My arms were covered in thick brown fur.

I dropped back into the armchair. "Uh ...
Doctor Grendel," I said, "can we talk?"

# EPILOGUE FROM SLAPPY

Haha. It's cold up on that mountaintop. Looks like Judy won't be needing a fur coat this winter!

What's that old saying? "The family that howls together, prowls together." Or something like that. Hahaha.

I'd love to see Ira and Judy's next game of Slap Tag. Bet it will be a SCREAM! Hahaha.

That's our story for this time.

Let's all take a long run in the forest to clear our heads. Then I'll be back with another *Goosebumps* story.

Remember, this is *SlappyWorld*.

You only *scream* in it!

## SLAPPYWORLD #16:
## SLAPPY IN DREAMLAND

## Read on for a preview!

Slappy stared across the table at me. His eyes gleamed under the lamp light, and his red-lipped grin made him look like he was happy to be here.

Maybe you'll think I'm weird. But that ventriloquist dummy is my best friend. Ever since Dad gave him to me for my twelfth birthday, we've been pals.

I keep Slappy with me wherever I go. I even took him to school once. Mom warned me not to, and she was right. Some kids in my class laughed at me and made jokes about how I must be a dummy, too.

Not funny.

My name is Richard Hsieh, and I'm really not a weird dude. The truth is, I've always wanted a pet, and I'm allergic to dogs and cats.

So I guess Slappy takes the place of a pet for me.

My family moved to Russet Village less than a year ago, and I started at Russet Middle School last September. So I haven't had time to make real friends.

And I have to admit something about me. I'm shy. When I started at the new school, I had to fill out a questionnaire. You know. A lot of questions about what I like to do and what I don't like.

At the bottom, it said: Can you describe yourself in one word?

And that's what I wrote— *shy*.

I was going to write *awesome*. Just as a joke. But I thought whoever read my answers might take it seriously and think I'm stuck-up.

I looked at Slappy. Then down at the table.

I was doing a thousand-piece jigsaw puzzle with black-and-white pandas on it—no color— so it was really hard. "It's almost done. Only twelve pieces to go," I said.

Slappy grinned back at me. I really wished he could talk.

Dad keeps telling me to stop talking to the dummy all the time. He thinks it's too weird.

But Mom is a doctor, and she doesn't see any problem with it. "Lots of kids have imaginary friends they talk to," she told Dad.

"Sure. When they are *three*," Dad shot back.

"He can talk to Slappy all he wants," Mom said. "It's not like Richard imagines that Slappy is alive."

Dad shrugged, blew out a long whoosh of air, and left the room.

Dad is manager of the hardware store in town. A few days before my birthday, he found a beat-up suitcase in the back room of the store. He opened the case and found Slappy folded up inside it.

The dummy's gray suit was wrinkled, and his wooden head had scratches on it and a tiny chip missing from his lower lip. Dad asked the other store workers if they knew who had left the dummy there. No one had a clue.

So that's how Slappy became my birthday gift.

Mom and Dad washed him up before they let me have him. "He probably has lice or something," Dad said.

"What an evil grin," Mom said.

"It is *not* an evil grin," I said. "He's just smiling."

"It looks like he's smiling about something evil," Mom said. "Maybe you can practice with him, Richard. Practice making him talk. Work up a comedy act. That might be fun."

"I . . . I'm not very good with jokes," I told her.

Mom frowned at me. "But it might help build up your confidence," she said.

I wasn't sure about that. But I did like having Slappy with me. And maybe I did talk to him too often. But so what?

I had been staring at the black-and-white jigsaw puzzle so long, my eyes were starting to go blurry. "Just a few more pieces," I told Slappy.

But I felt a hand on my shoulder. "Get your coat, Richard," Mom said. "Dinner ran so long, we're late."

I looked up from the pandas. "Late?"

"Did you forget? You're coming with me to my lab tonight. It's Bring-Your-Kid-To-Work day."

I dropped the puzzle piece in my hand and jumped up from the table. "Sorry, Mom. I'll get my coat."

"And how about some shoes?" she said. "Shoes might be good."

I hurried to my room to get my sneakers.

Mom runs a sleep lab at the hospital. I guess people who have trouble sleeping come to her lab. I've never been there before.

I tied my sneakers. Then I pulled my jacket out of the front closet. "Is it okay if I bring Slappy?" I asked.

Mom squinted at me. "Slappy?"

"Yes. Is it okay if I bring him?"

She thought about it for a moment. "Sure," she said. "Bring him along. The more the merrier."

And that's when all the trouble started.

2

Mom's sleep lab has its own entrance at the side of the hospital. We walked down a brightly lit hallway. Then Mom pushed open the doors to the lab.

I blinked as my eyes adjusted to the dim gray light. I saw dark curtains and narrow beds and lots of computer equipment. The curtains formed a row of bedrooms, with a bed and a computer in each room.

People were already here. Some sat on their beds. Three of them stood in a corner, talking. They were all dressed in pajamas and robes. They turned as Mom and I walked in.

"Sorry I'm late," Mom said. "This is my son Richard. And that thing he has draped over his shoulder is his dummy friend Slappy."

"Slappy might give me nightmares!" a man called from one of the beds.

A few people laughed. Most of them looked pretty old to me. But I saw a couple of younger people, too.

"Don't say that," Mom said. "This is a No Nightmare zone, remember?"

A young man in a white lab uniform appeared from a back room. He was tall and thin and had dark eyes and straight black hair pulled behind his head in a short ponytail.

"Hello, Doctor," he said. "This must be your son."

Mom introduced me and Slappy. "Richard, this is Salazar, my assistant," she said. "Salazar does all the hard work here. I just watch everyone sleep."

He chuckled. "Your mom is being modest," he said. He turned to my mother. "Only six here tonight. Mrs. Baker couldn't come in. I was just about to hook everyone up."

"I'll put Slappy in my office," Mom said. She pointed to the back room. Through the big window, I could see rows of computer monitors. "Then you can watch Salazar hook up the patients. He can explain what we do here."

She lifted Slappy off my shoulder. "Wow. He's heavier than I thought."

The dummy's eyelids lowered. I laughed. "Slappy knows he's in a sleep lab!"

Shaking her head, Mom had to carry him in both hands.

"Bedtime, everyone!" Salazar called out. "Settle in, and I'll get you ready. You all know the routine."

In their curtained-off rooms, the patients

climbed into their beds. They all stayed on their backs on top of the covers.

Salazar gave them time to get into place. "What grade are you in, Richard?" he asked.

"Sixth," I said.

"And are you interested in anything particular? Think you might like to be a doctor like your mom?"

I shrugged. "I don't really know," I muttered.

I hate it when people ask me what I want to be. I know Salazar was just trying to be nice. But I never know what to say. I mean, I'm only a kid. How do I know what I want to do with the rest of my life?

"You brought that old ventriloquist dummy," he said. "Are you interested in puppets?"

"Not really," I said.

He nodded. "Well, follow me. We'll start with Mister Baldwin." He led the way to the first bed.

Mr. Baldwin was an older guy with a fringe of white hair around his head and a short white beard that covered most of his face. He wore a black nightshirt and black socks.

He squinted at me. "Are you Salazar's new assistant?"

Salazar answered for me. "It's Bring-Your-Kid-to-Work Day at the hospital," he said. "Richard has never seen what his mother does."

"She watches us sleep all night," Mr. Baldwin said. "I don't know how *she* manages to stay awake!"

"Are you feeling sleepy tonight, Mr. Baldwin?"

He groaned. "I feel tired all the time," he said. "Except at bedtime."

"We'll see how you do tonight," Salazar told him. He lifted a bunch of wires from the computer table beside the bed. "These are electrodes, Richard. We attach them to Mr. Baldwin, and they transmit his sleep patterns to the little monitors beside each bed—and to the big monitors in your mother's office."

He dipped an electrode into a gooey liquid and stuck it onto one side of Mr. Baldwin's forehead. Then he attached a second electrode to the other side of the forehead.

"There are eight electrodes in all," Salazar explained to me.

"Did you ever see the movie *Frankenstein*?" Mr. Baldwin asked me. "That's what this looks like. It's what they did to the Frankenstein monster."

Salazar attached a few more electrodes. "There isn't anything scary about it," he said. "It allows us to see how deep Mr. Baldwin's sleep is, when he wakes up, when he dreams, anything that interrupts his sleep."

"Can you see his dreams?" I asked.

Salazar shook his head. "No. Only *when* he dreams, not *what* he dreams."

He hooked up the eighth electrode. "Pleasant dreams," he said. "I'll turn off all the lights when I get everyone online."

I followed him into the next curtained bedroom. Salazar talked quietly with all the patients as he attached the electrodes to them. Some of them appeared sleepy, but some seemed wide awake.

I wondered if I could fall asleep with all those wires connected to my skin. That might be hard. And, I wondered how my mom stayed awake all night, watching the sleep patterns of six patients.

Salazar hooked up the last patient and pointed to the back room. "You can go see your mom now, Richard," he said. "She'll show you what she watches on the computer monitors."

I nodded and started to the office. On the way, I had an idea.

It was a funny idea. "Mom, I want to try hooking electrodes to someone," I said.

Mom laughed. "Why? Did that look like fun to you? It isn't as easy as it seems. They have to go in exactly the right place."

"I just want to try," I said. I picked up Slappy. "Can I try it on him? Can I hook up Slappy?"

She squinted at me. "Seriously?"

I nodded. "Come on. Let me try."

"Okay," she said. "Why not? Follow me."

I slung Slappy over my shoulder and followed Mom to one of the empty beds. "Put him down here on his back," she said.

I settled him on the bed. His eyes stayed closed, as if he was already asleep.

Mom arranged the wires and electrodes on the table beside the bed. She opened a tube of the gooey stuff and poured it into a small bowl. "Okay, go ahead," she said. "Dip the electrode into the gel and attach it to Slappy."

I did it just the way I had watched Salazar work. I stuck a wire on each side of Slappy's forehead. Then two on his neck. Three on his chest. And one on top of his head.

"Okay. Good job," Mom said. She turned and fiddled with the computer monitor on the table. "Let's see what we've got."

We both gazed at the screen as it came to life.

Suddenly, Mom's eyes went wide and she let out a loud gasp. "Whaaaat!" she cried. "I don't *believe* it!"

# 3

"Mom—what's wrong?" I cried.

She blinked several times and then squinted at the wiggly yellow lines going across the monitor.

"This . . . this doesn't make any sense!" Mom stammered. "I'm seeing *brain activity*. But that's *impossible!* That can't happen with a lifeless dummy."

Mom stared at the monitor. I heard a loud blip, and then a crackling sound. Like an electric shock.

The jagged yellow lines rolled across the screen. Then she gazed down at Slappy again. "Impossible," she murmured.

"I . . . I don't understand," I stammered. "Why are you upset?"

"Because a wooden dummy can't send out brain signals," she answered. "Look at the lines on the screen. You have to be *alive* to send out those brain waves."

# About the Author

R.L. Stine says he gets to scare people all over the world. So far, his books have sold more than 400 million copies, making him one of the most popular children's authors in history. The Goosebumps series has more than 150 titles and has inspired a TV series and two motion pictures. R.L. himself is a character in the movies! He has also written the teen series Fear Street, and the Mostly Ghostly and Nightmare Room series. He is currently writing a series of graphic novels entitled Just Beyond. R.L. Stine lives in New York City with his wife, Jane, an editor and publisher. You can learn more about him at rlstine.com.

# Catch the
# MOST WANTED
# Goosebumps® villains
# UNDEAD OR ALIVE!

## SPECIAL EDITIONS

■ SCHOLASTIC
scholastic.com/goosebumps

GBMW42

**REVENGE OF THE LIVING DUMMY**
**R.L. STINE**
SCHOLASTIC

**CREEP FROM THE DEEP**
**R.L. STINE**
SCHOLASTIC

**MONSTER BLOOD FOR BREAKFAST!**
**R.L. STINE**
SCHOLASTIC

**THE SCREAM OF THE HAUNTED MASK**
**R.L. STINE**
SCHOLASTIC

**DR. MANIAC VS. ROBBY SCHWARTZ**
**R.L. STINE**
SCHOLASTIC

**WHO'S YOUR MUMMY?**
**R.L. STINE**
SCHOLASTIC

**MY FRIENDS CALL ME MONSTER**
**R.L. STINE**
SCHOLASTIC

**SAY CHEESE - AND DIE SCREAMING!**
**R.L. STINE**
SCHOLASTIC

**WELCOME TO CAMP SLITHER**
**R.L. STINE**
SCHOLASTIC

SCHOLASTIC

www.scholastic.com/goosebumps

GBHL19H2

# THE SCARIEST PLACE ON EARTH!

HELP! WE HAVE STRANGE POWERS!
R.L. STINE

ESCAPE FROM HORRORLAND
R.L. STINE

THE STREETS OF PANIC PARK
R.L. STINE

WHEN THE GHOST DOG HOWLS
R.L. STINE

LITTLE SHOP OF HAMSTERS
R.L. STINE

HEADS, YOU LOSE!
R.L. STINE

WEIRDO HALLOWEEN
R.L. STINE

THE WIZARD OF OOZE
R.L. STINE

SLAPPY NEW YEAR!
R.L. STINE

THE HORROR AT CHILLER HOUSE
R.L. STINE

# The Original Bone-Chilling Series

 ®

—with Exclusive
Author Interviews!

# R. L. Stine's Fright Fest!
## Now with Splat Stats and More!

# CONTINUE THE FRIGHT
## AT THE GOOSEBUMPS SITE
# scholastic.com/goosebumps

## FANS OF GOOSEBUMPS CAN:

- PLAY THE GHOULISH GAME:
  GOOSEBUMPS: SLAPPY'S DROP DEAD HOUSE

- LEARN ABOUT NEW BOOKS AND TERRIFYING CLASSICS

- TAKE A QUIZ AND LEARN WHICH TYPE OF MONSTER YOU ARE!

- LEARN ABOUT THE AUTHOR WHO STARTED IT ALL: R.L. STINE

**■ SCHOLASTIC**

GBWEB2019

# THE GOOSEBUMPS SERIES COMES TO LIFE IN A BRAND-NEW DIGITAL WORLD

**MEET** Slappy—and explore the Goosebumps Zone.
**PLAY** games, create an avatar, and chat with other fans.

Start your adventure today! Download the **HOME BASE** app and scan this image to unlock exclusive rewards!

## SCHOLASTIC.COM/HOMEBASE

**SCHOLASTIC**

# Goosebumps

# SLAPPYWORLD

## THIS IS SLAPPY'S WORLD—
## YOU ONLY SCREAM IN IT!

**SLAPPY BIRTHDAY TO YOU**
R.L. STINE

**ATTACK OF THE JACK!**
R.L. STINE

**I AM SLAPPY'S EVIL TWIN**
R.L. STINE

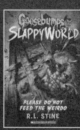

**PLEASE DO NOT FEED THE WEIRDO**
R.L. STINE

**ESCAPE FROM SHUDDER MANSION**
R.L. STINE

**THE GHOST OF SLAPPY**
R.L. STINE

**IT'S ALIVE! IT'S ALIVE!**
R.L. STINE

**THE DUMMY MEETS THE MUMMY!**
R.L. STINE

**REVENGE OF THE INVISIBLE BOY!**
R.L. STINE

**DIARY OF A DUMMY**
R.L. STINE

**THEY CALL ME THE NIGHT HOWLER!**
R.L. STINE

**MY FRIEND SLAPPY**
R.L. STINE

**MONSTER BLOOD IS BACK**
R.L. STINE

**FIFTH-GRADE ZOMBIES**
R.L. STINE

**JUDY AND THE BEAST**
R.L. STINE

**SCHOLASTIC**

GBSLAPPYWORLD15